Ski . . . or die.

Patrick guided Theresa in between trees, over moguls that nearly threw them both in the air, and down a mountain that Theresa couldn't have skied alone without serious injury. Patrick made her feel as if she could do anything.

Several more shots rang out.

Something whizzed over Theresa's head.

"That was too close!" she called.

"We need speed!" he yelled back.

He suddenly crouched in front of her and slowed down. *Slowed down?*

"Patrick, what are you—*whoaaa!*"

When he slowed, Theresa bumped into him, almost flipping right over his head. Just then he stood up sharply on his skis. Theresa felt her body lift with his. Her skis left the snow.

She was riding him piggyback.

Don't miss any books in this thrilling new series:

#1 *License to Thrill*
#2 *Live and Let Spy*
#3 *Nobody Does It Better*
#4 *Spy Girls Are Forever*
#5 *Dial "V" for Vengeance* *
#6 *If Looks Could Kill* *

Available from ARCHWAY Paperbacks

* Coming soon

Spy
Girls Are
Forever

by
Elizabeth Cage

AN ARCHWAY PAPERBACK
Published by POCKET BOOKS
New York   London   Toronto   Sydney   Tokyo   Singapore

AN ARCHWAY PAPERBACK *Original*

An Archway Paperback published by
POCKET BOOKS, a division of Simon & Schuster Inc.
1230 Avenue of the Americas, New York, NY 10020

Spy Girls™ is a trademark of Daniel Weiss Associates, Inc.

Produced by 17th Street Productions,
a division of Daniel Weiss Associates, Inc.
33 West 17th Street, New York, NY 10011

Copyright © 1999 by 17th Street Productions,
a division of Daniel Weiss Associates, Inc.
Cover art copyright © 1999 by 17th Street Productions,
a division of Daniel Weiss Associates, Inc.

ISBN: 0-671-02289-X

First Archway Paperback printing March 1999

10 9 8 7 6 5 4 3 2 1

AN ARCHWAY PAPERBACK and colophon are registered trademarks of Simon & Schuster Inc.

Printed in the U.S.A.

IL 7+

To Sean, George, Roger, Timothy, and Pierce—
a few good men who know a Spy Girl
when they see one.

Beam me out of here," Jo Carreras muttered as she and Theresa Hearth entered the now familiar white plastic conference room of The Tower for another debriefing. "This place needs a major makeover. The latter-day mother ship motif is *way* out."

"Tell it to Uncle Sam," Theresa replied. She gently set her laptop on the pristine white conference table that stretched the length of the entire room. It had to be at least twenty feet long. "Maybe he'll turn you loose with The Tower platinum card."

"Yeah, right. Only if we save the world just one more time." Jo flipped her long black hair out of her face. Then she snatched a blueberry muffin from a small tray of juice, bagels, muffins, and other breakfast treats in the center of the conference table. The tray was the only thing in the room that hinted at warmth. Let alone humanity.

Actually, there was a time when the sight of

this conference room/bad *Trek* set creeped Jo and Theresa out. Now it wasn't eerie so much as tacky. But back then, they were just raw recruits thrown together to save the Free World from Evil and other capitalized words. They'd been so green when the organization known only as The Tower had trained them as secret agents.

Naturally, their enemies underestimated three teenage girls. But the adventures had been intense. Dangerous. Thrilling. Terrifying. And exhausting. They had defused bombs, fallen out of airplanes, hacked into top secret computers, run from the law, and trotted the globe using false identities. They had used gadgets that would make James Bond drool. They wore fabulous couture that would make him drool even more. Soon they stopped being just girls.

They became the Spy Girls.

Jo glanced around and blinked her large ebony eyes. "Where's Caylin?"

Theresa shrugged.

Then they heard a high-pitched *"Kiii-yai!"*

The door at the opposite end of the room flew open, and Caylin Pike burst in, blond ponytail flipping, fists wrapped in athletic tape. She danced back and forth, boxing the air and twirling while she executed a series of wicked roundhouse kicks.

"It's about time," Jo murmured.

Caylin whooshed past Theresa and headed toward Jo's seat. She punched with each step— "Ya! Ya! Ya!"—all the way up to Jo. Then Caylin launched a final sidekick that came within an inch of Jo's nose.

"Now *that's* what I'm talking about." Caylin grinned, holding the foot in front of Jo's face. Jo didn't even flinch—except to wrinkle her nose.

"Ever hear of foot-odor spray?" she asked.

Caylin swung her foot back to the ground and stood in place. Her shoulders slumped. "I do *not* stink!"

"Your feet do," Jo replied with a wry smile.

Caylin ignored her, choosing instead to plop her foot on the conference table, bend forward, and stretch her hamstring. "This tae-bo stuff is unreal. It's total body kamikaze. You guys have to try it. You'll die."

"Just what I want out of a workout," Theresa said.

"No thanks, Van Damage," Jo added. "You work out enough for all of us."

"You don't even know what working out is," Caylin scolded, massaging her calf. She paused to snag a bottle of water from the tray.

"Working out?" Theresa asked, looking confused. She turned to Jo, shrugging. "Never heard of it."

"You know, weights, treadmills, ambulances," Jo quipped. "You've seen the infomercials."

Theresa widened her gray eyes in mock surprise. *"That's* working out? Ew!"

"God forbid you break a sweat," Caylin grumbled.

"You break the sweats, I'll break the codes," Theresa replied, patting her laptop.

"So what does Jo break?" Caylin asked.

Theresa grinned. "Wind."

"Hey!" Jo erupted, throwing a muffin. It exploded against Theresa's arm, sending chunky crumbs across the spotless white table. "You're supposed to be the quiet one!"

"You should try quiet sometime," Theresa said with a laugh, brushing crumbs away.

"Very funny," Jo said with an exaggerated toss of her dark hair. "The only thing I break is hearts, Spy Geek. Don't you forget it."

"Yeah, I heard that enemies of state all over the world are paying big bucks for the latest satellite pics of you sunbathing on The Tower roof," Caylin pointed out.

Jo blinked. "They are?"

Caylin and Theresa exploded in giggles and groans. "Yeah, *right!"*

Jo sighed melodramatically and shook her head. "It's so hard being beautiful, brilliant, and top secret."

"Ahem," came a deep voice from all around them, as if from within the walls.

The Spy Girls froze.

"Uh-oh," Caylin said, glancing about. "The Sam-man cometh. Cease all fun."

The lights dimmed. A large video screen emerged from the far wall, blinking and humming. Gradually the pixelated image of Uncle Sam, their boss, came to life before them. As usual, they couldn't make out any of his features.

"Greetings, Spy Girls," Uncle Sam said. "How are the debutantes of détente today?"

"My word, Uncle Sam," Jo gasped. "What have you done with your face?"

"I always look like this, Jo," Uncle Sam replied.

Jo rolled her eyes. "That was a joke. You know—what have you done with your face . . . like, 'where is it?'"

"I know what you meant, Jo," Uncle Sam replied dryly. "Do you think you're the first operative to come up with that one?"

"Oooh, have some, Spy Girl!" Caylin whispered.

"Yeah, yeah, yeah," Jo grumbled. "Dish it, Sammy. What's this week's crisis?"

"Well, it's a crisis, all right," Uncle Sam replied. "But it's a little different this time out."

"Different?" Theresa asked.

"Let me guess," Jo interjected. "Forty nuclear warheads have been stolen from Russia, and we have to infiltrate the Moscow mob. Dressed as nuns."

"No, that's not it," Caylin said. "We have to go to Nepal to rescue the Dalai Lama from a band of rebel Sherpas."

"Dressed as nuns," Jo repeated.

"If you two are finished?" Uncle Sam replied coldly.

"We have to go up in the space shuttle!" Caylin went on.

"Go undercover as Dallas Cowboy cheerleaders!" Jo countered.

"Now *that* would be cool," Caylin agreed.

"That's *quite* enough!" Uncle Sam exclaimed.

The girls paused, staring at the screen. Finally Jo muttered, "He is *so* decaf this morning."

"As I was saying when I was so *rudely* interrupted," Uncle Sam continued, "your next mission is a bit different. I assume you are all familiar with the Mediterranean principality Zagaria, along with its royal family."

"Princess Kristal," Theresa replied.

"Correct. The eighteen-year-old princess. Her mother, Queen Cascadia. And Prince Arthur, who just turned fifteen."

"Lucky kid," Caylin commented. "That's big bucks."

"Who'd want to be a royal?" Theresa scoffed. "Talk about lack of free will."

"Funny you should say that, Theresa," Uncle Sam said. "Because it's exactly free will that has the palace in an uproar. It seems Kristal has been exercising her free will a little too freely these days."

"How so?" Caylin asked.

"Let me guess," Jo piped up. "It has something to do with her boyfriend, Rook."

"Exactly," Uncle Sam replied. "How did you know?"

Jo smiled. "I read the newspapers."

"Ha!" Theresa replied. "Like the *International Trasher*?"

Jo scowled. "That's *Tracker*, giga-girl! If you spoke any language other than Java, you'd *know* that it keeps its finger on the pulse of pop culture like no other newspaper."

"At a second-grade reading level," Theresa argued. "There's not enough soap in the cheesiest of operas to wash the dirt out of *that* rag."

"Ladies!" Uncle Sam said. "If I may?"

Jo and Theresa fell silent.

"Here's the situation: Kristal has run off to Schnell to do a little skiing in the Swiss Alps. The royal family is fairly certain that Rook is with her. Queen Cascadia fears that this could lead to more complicated—and permanent—romantic matters."

"Like marriage?" Caylin offered.

"Like marriage," Uncle Sam confirmed. "It's no secret the queen doesn't like Rook. If Kristal and Rook marry, the implications for the monarchy would be huge. Her Majesty has requested that The Tower locate the princess and return her to Zagaria."

"Schnell," Jo said in awe. "That's the most exclusive ski resort in Europe."

"With the best snowboarding in the world," Caylin added.

Theresa shook her head at her comrades' enthusiasm. "Doesn't the royal fam have bodyguards to handle this kind of stuff? I mean, why do *we* have to go?"

"Are you nuts, Theresa?" Jo demanded. "This is a cakewalk right into the jaws of luxury. It's *Schnell!*"

"The point, Theresa," Uncle Sam replied, "is that Kristal doesn't want to be found. Surely you know her reputation. She'd rather be the rock star that she is than a princess. She and Rook have been on the front cover of every tabloid in the world. This is her way of rebelling against her upbringing. Schnell isn't that big a town, but there are many intimate places for a girl like Kristal to hide. She goes there often, so she must have dependable people willing to keep her whereabouts discreet for a bribe. She would see royal bodyguards coming a mile away. On the other hand, three American girls who are fans just might be able to get close to her."

"Skiing and jet-setting," Caylin mused. "Sounds like a choice little mission."

"My advice would be to follow the paparazzi," Uncle Sam suggested. "They know the clubs where Kristal has been giving surprise concerts."

"Cool," Jo said.

"Lame," Theresa countered.

"What's your malfunction?" Jo asked. "Nothing's going to blow up, no one's going to die, and the world is still safe for democracy."

"That's the point," Theresa replied. "Shouldn't we be doing something a little more challenging? We've proven ourselves. Isn't there a *real* crisis out there somewhere?"

"Yeah, in your head," Jo muttered.

"I'm serious."

"T., we couldn't ask for a better mission." Caylin paused. "Actually, after our little fiasco in Seattle, we very well *should* ask for a better mission."

"Ask and ye shall receive," Uncle Sam said. "Theresa, relax and enjoy this one. If you pull it off, there's a whole week of rest and relaxation in Schnell for the three of you, courtesy of the royal family and The Tower."

"Are you kidding?" Jo squealed. "That is totally Gandhi of you, Uncle Sam! I take back all the things I said about your face!"

"Thank you, Jo," Uncle Sam replied. "But there is one thing. . . ."

"Uh-oh," Caylin moaned.

"Oh no," Theresa breathed.

"What, pray tell?" Jo asked.

The pixels in Uncle Sam's image multiplied into a mischievous smile. "You have to find the princess in seventy-two hours."

Theresa snorted. "Three days? Yeah. Okay. Sure. Nothing like chasing a spoiled brat through a maze of clubs full of Euro-snobs smoking cigarettes that cost more than my haircut."

"We'll do it," Jo declared.

"No problem," Caylin agreed. "Sorry, T. You might actually have to go outdoors on this one."

"Ha ha," Theresa replied. She glumly raised her glass of orange juice. "Here's to world peace."

"Nah, here's to cool slopes and hot tubs," Jo shot back.

"Good luck, Spy Girls," Uncle Sam declared. "I'll contact you when you reach your home base in Schnell. I think you'll find your accommodations quite . . . accommodating."

Caylin stood and raised her drink as well. "Let's rock and roll, ladies!"

Two juice glasses and one water bottle clicked together. And then the Spy Girls were off.

2

I don't think I've ever seen snow so white," Jo marveled as she and her compatriots arrived at the front door of their base of operations. It was a stunning A-frame at the base of the mountain, only a few hundred yards from the Schnell Ski Lodge. They literally could ski right to their front door.

The Alps surrounded them, as tall as the sky and covered with a fresh blanket of snow from the night before. Schnell was nestled in a remote valley in Switzerland, a quaint collection of old-country buildings combined with state-of-the-art resort fare. You could get Swiss chocolate on one corner, a mud bath on another, and a confidential bank account on yet another. Everything in the town was designed to cater to the rich and foreign. Charm might have been Schnell's first name, but money was its middle.

And here the Spy Girls were, in front of one of the choicest chalets in the valley.

"Okay, guys, it's four o'clock," Theresa announced

after the Schnell clock tower chimed four times. "Uncle Sam told us that'd be our official mission kick-off time. Time's running out!"

"Oh, stop, Nervous Nellie," Caylin said with a laugh. "Wow, you can actually smell how clean the air is up here." She took a deep breath. "Man, I can't wait to hit the slopes."

"Why don't we hit the house first," Theresa suggested grumpily, shifting her bags on her shoulders. "I'd like to put this gear down sometime before the millennium."

Caylin rolled her baby blues and fished an electronic key card out of her pocket. She slid it into a slot by the doorknob, and the door opened. "Maybe you shouldn't bring so many computers, T."

"Really," Jo agreed. "Does Bill Gates know you stole his mainframe?"

"Someone has to do the homework," Theresa replied.

"I did all the homework we need on the plane," Jo declared, brandishing a copy of the latest *International Tracker*. "Now it's time to *west* and *welax.*"

She nudged the door open with her foot, and the trio entered what was going to be their home for the next three days—and hopefully the week after that.

Jaws dropped all around.

"Holy Richie Rich, Batman," Jo whispered. "Can you say, 'Cinderella'?"

"Do you realize that you just subreferenced three cartoon characters in one sentence?" Theresa mumbled, her voice full of awe at the sight before her.

"Who cares," Jo replied dreamily.

The roof of the A-frame rose to a point three stories above their heads, all of it immaculate, dark-stained wood. Several ceiling fans spun, lazily moving the toasty-warm air. A spiral staircase led to the second and third floors. To the right was a kitchen fit for a chef. To the left, a roaring fire was set in a magnificent stone fireplace that was big enough to stand in. And straight ahead? A wall of glass facing the mountain, one of the most spectacular views the girls had ever seen.

Caylin dumped her bag and broke for the almost invisible glass doors, which opened out onto the backyard. Theresa was mesmerized by the wall of gadgetry in the entertainment center. Jo simply drifted to the center of the room and spun, staring at the ceiling.

"I can't believe this," Theresa gushed, indexing the array of electronic hardware that surrounded the giant screen TV. "CD, DVD, DAT, HDTV, and the new MONDO-SAT system that allows access to every single television station in the world." She hefted a remote control that had more buttons than the cockpit of a 747. "Jo, do you realize that we can watch *Party of Five* reruns in Finnish, Russian, and Swahili *simultaneously?*"

It was as if Theresa hadn't even spoken. Jo just whispered, "It's not fair. How are we supposed to complete the mission in three days when we can't even bear to leave the house? I mean, think of the party we could have tonight!"

Behind her, the sliding glass door flew open. Caylin stomped in, huffing clouds of breath. She appeared to be in a daze, as if she'd just been hit on the head. "There is a hot tub out here. You can do *laps* in it. I mean, this is a serious hot tub. I've never seen a hot tub like this. We're talking a hot tub big enough for Rook's entire entourage."

Theresa had torn one of her laptops from its nylon case and was feverishly plugging in adapters to the rear of one of the electronic components. "I could break into the Pentagon with this stuff."

"I checked out the backyard, too," Caylin said. "There's a garage back there. Ask me what's in it."

Jo's eyes locked on Caylin's like lasers. "What's in it?"

"Snowmobiles."

Jo let out a high-pitched squeak. "Did you see the make?"

"Does 'Snownuke 667' sound right?"

Jo screamed and launched herself at the doors. She disappeared in a fluff of snow.

"This is ridiculous," Caylin grumbled, some of the excitement wearing off. "This is the coolest pad The Tower's given us yet. How are we supposed to concentrate on our mission with all these distractions?"

Theresa stopped fussing with wires and gazed at her friend. "Maybe that's the point. Maybe this is a test."

"Give us a cream puff mission with a time limit, and see how professional we are?"

Theresa shrugged. "Makes sense."

Caylin sighed and slumped into one of the stunning leather sofas. "I think we'd better get out of here tonight and search for Kristal before we do anything else. I mean, don't even unpack."

"Good idea," Theresa replied. "That sounds like a plan."

"Promise we won't let each other slack?" Caylin offered.

Theresa marched over to Caylin and held out her hand. They shook. "Promise. Spy Girls get the job done."

"Yes, ma'am."

Just then they heard a roar outside. Jo ripped

by on a sleek black Snownuke, her fist raised in the air. White chunks spun up from the snow-mobile's track, and they heard a distinct *"yeeeeeee-haaaaaaa!"* before Jo disappeared around the corner.

Theresa sighed. "This is definitely going to be harder than we thought."

The Schnell Ski Lodge was far more than just a ski lodge. It was a full-fledged resort with conference areas, two nightclubs, six restaurants, and a five-star hotel. People of all nationalities roamed the hallways, some dressed for skiing, some dressed for dinner, some dressed strictly for business.

"This is wrong," Caylin said as the trio wandered through the complex. "Kristal is a world-wide celebrity. She wouldn't be caught dead just walking around here."

"I agree," Theresa replied. "There're too many people around. Someone would spot her, and the jig would be up."

"Not to mention the crowd that would form," Caylin added. "She'd be mobbed."

"Do you have any suggestions?" Jo said.

"We need information," Theresa commented. "We need to know where she's been, what clubs she's hit, and then—"

Theresa's mouth dropped open.

"T.?" Caylin asked. "What's wrong?"

"No way," Theresa said incredulously. "No way. Nuh-uh. Can't be."

"*What?*" Jo demanded.

"Dr. Eve is here!"

Jo and Caylin shared a clueless look. "Who?"

"Dr. Eve!" Theresa replied. "She's giving a lecture at eight. What time is it?"

"Quarter to," Jo replied.

"Oh, man, we have to go. We just *have* to. It'll be so cool, guys, seriously. You *have* to go with me!"

"Whoa," Caylin said, holding up her hands. "Who is Dr. Eve, and tell me again what you think we should be doing?"

"Is she like Dr. Ruth?" Jo asked.

Theresa moaned and rolled her eyes. "She's only one of the foremost female scientists in the world! She won the Nobel Prize for her work in space."

"She's an astronaut?" asked Caylin.

"Cosmonaut," Theresa corrected. "She's Russian. Her full name is Dr. Eve Dankanov, but she just calls herself Dr. Eve. She lived on a space station for over a year. She's one of my idols. We *have* to go see her."

"Uh, hello?" Caylin scolded. "Weren't *you* the one saying that we should concentrate on the mission? We have three days to find Kristal. And that's it."

"This won't take *that* long," Theresa pleaded. "An hour, tops. If you're bored, you can leave. In fact, forget it. I'll go alone."

"We shouldn't split up yet," Caylin warned. "We don't know this place well enough. What do you think, Jo?"

"I think those two guys are staring at us," Jo replied, gazing across the lobby.

They weren't just guys—they were identical twins. Tall, dark, unbelievably foxy identical twins. And they were definitely staring at the Spy Girls.

"I think I'm in love," Jo said huskily. "Wow. Double your pleasure, double your fun. Two great tastes that go great together. Two all-beef patties, special sauce, lettuce, cheese—"

"What are you, a walking jingle machine?" Theresa asked impatiently. "Come on! *What's the plan, people?*"

Jo tensed. "They're coming this way!" She quickly ran her hands through her hair. "How do I look?"

"Terrible!" Caylin said in mock disgust. "How do you face the mirror every morning?"

As the twins approached, their features became clearer—and they became even more handsome. They had thick dark hair that was tousled and spiky. They had deep-set brown eyes that seemed to pierce whatever they looked at and chiseled features right out of a couture ad. They dressed all in black: black turtlenecks, black sport coats, and black slacks. The only hints of color were the bloodred silk handkerchiefs in each of their breast pockets.

"*Buona sera,* signorinas," one twin said, extending his hand. "I am Santino. You are American?"

Jo stepped forward and shook his hand, which was strong and warm. A chill went through her. "Yes, American." She flashed a sexy little grin. "And you're Italian."

"*Sì,*" said the talking twin. "This is my brother, Carlo. We're twins."

Jo's eyes lit up. "Really? You're kidding. That's so cool."

"Oh, can it, Scarlett," Caylin growled, stepping forward. "I'm Cay—uh, Caroline. This is . . ."

"Tish," Theresa chimed in.

"Yeah, Tish. And this," Caylin said, referring grandly to Jo, "is *Joan.*"

Jo shot Caylin a venomous look over her shoulder. "*Joan?*" she mouthed in disgust.

"Hello to you all, ladies," Santino said. "You are here for Dr. Eve's speech, I hope?"

"Yes," Theresa said immediately. "We wouldn't miss it for the world."

"You follow her work, then?"

"I do," Theresa replied. "These two just kind of—"

"*Of course* we follow her work," Jo interrupted.

"I've always found it fascinating how someone can live for such a long time in a weightless environment."

"You mean like in your head?" Theresa muttered.

Jo ignored her. "It looks crowded. I hope we can get a seat."

"Have no fear," Santino replied. "Carlo and I work for Dr. Eve. We're her assistants. We can see to it that you have seats in the front row. That is, if you don't mind sitting next to us?"

"I don't mind a bit," Jo said. "You don't mind, do you, ladies?"

"Guess not," Caylin said, resigned. She caught the silent Carlo staring at her. She smiled, and he looked away.

"Carlo is a little shy," Santino said, giving his brother a playful tap on the head. "He doesn't talk."

"Much," Carlo added with a slight smile.

"What do you say, signorinas?" Santino asked. "Shall we take our seats?"

"Cool," Theresa said. "Let's go."

As they entered the auditorium Caylin snagged Theresa's arm and pulled her close. "Shoot. I *totally* blanked on the alias thing," she whispered. "I just . . . improvised. Think we're okay?"

"I guess so," Theresa replied. "I'm sure the

Wonder Twins here wouldn't know the difference if you'd said you were Caylin, Caroline, or Captain Kirk. I'm sure Uncle Sam will understand."

"If you say so. I know better than to ask Jo when there's flirting to be done, but what about the stupid mission?"

"We're here—let's just go with it," Theresa said. "We can scour the clubs for Kristal afterward. But I've been dying to see Dr. Eve forever. She's my idol. Besides, I think Carlo likes you."

Caylin smiled. "He is kind of cute. Well, they *both* are, but I tend to gravitate toward the strong, silent types."

"Hmmm. Looks like Jo thinks otherwise," Theresa said. "Check it out."

Jo already had her arm linked with Santino's as they strode down the auditorium aisle. She was animated and chatty—as always—and Santino was so smooth. Two master flirts doing what they did best.

Theresa felt a rush of adrenaline as the twins led them to the front row. She couldn't believe she was about to be *this close* to *the* Dr. Eve Dankanov!

They settled into their seats, and the twins excused themselves to make sure everything was in place.

"Isn't Santino a doll?" Jo gushed when they left. "I mean, did you see those eyes?"

"Yeah," Caylin replied. "Carlo has the same ones."

Theresa burst out laughing. The other two gaped at her.

"What's so funny?" Jo asked.

"You two," Theresa replied, trying unsuccessfully to hold in her giggles. "It's amazing what you guys will tolerate for a couple of chiseled chins. I mean, you guys *hate* the sciences—biological, physical, metaphysical—"

"Who's going to listen to the lecture?" Caylin retorted. "I couldn't care less about Dr. Eve."

"The only science I'm interested in is chemistry," Jo added. "And maybe the elements of attraction. Paramones."

"Pheromones." Theresa laughed again. "I hate to break the news to you, but these guys are probably borderline Ph.D.'s in astrophysics and mathematics. It might be a good idea to listen to the lecture so you don't sound like a couple of Beavises when they try to talk to you about it later."

Jo sighed and stared longingly at the curtain, behind which the twins had just disappeared. "T., I hate it when you're right."

"I don't mind it one bit," Theresa replied, smiling.

The lights dimmed and a hush came over the audience. Then Santino marched confidently on-stage to the podium. He politely tapped the mike to make sure it was on. *"Buona sera. Buenas noches. Guten Abend,"* he began, rattling off "good evening" in eight different languages, ending with English. "It gives me great pleasure to bring to the stage a true pioneer in astrophysics and zero gravity research. The Nobel Prize–winner and former cosmonaut commander, Dr. Eve Dankanov."

The auditorium erupted in applause. Theresa clapped violently and tried to stand, but Jo and Caylin yanked her back down into her seat.

Santino met up with Carlo at stage right, and the twins returned to their seats next to Jo and Caylin. Santino flashed a bright smile at Jo, who winked at him.

Theresa rolled her eyes.

Meanwhile, Dr. Eve marched proudly to the podium. She was a tall, powerfully built woman who obviously was used to being in charge. Her face was deathly pale and equally serious. Her jet black hair was pulled back in a bun so tight, it arched her eyebrows. Her ice blue eyes barely registered the crowd, focusing only on the podium and notes before her.

"Someone needs a makeover," Jo commented.

"Shhh!" Theresa scolded.

"In space, no one can hear you accessorize," Caylin prodded, referring to Dr. Eve's plain gray suit. There was no jewelry in sight. Not even earrings.

"She doesn't have time for *surface* stuff," Theresa stated. "She's far too busy with her work."

Jo sniffed.

Finally the applause died down and Dr. Eve greeted the crowd. Her voice was deep and commanding, and she spoke perfect English with just a touch of a Russian accent.

"Greetings, ladies and gentlemen, science symposium guests, and members of the press. I am Dr. Eve Dankanov. Tonight I wish to discuss Zimmerman's theories regarding the behavior of gas in a vacuum, such as space, versus its behavior in an atmosphere, such as the earth's. As some of you have guessed, I intend to expose Mr. Zimmerman's theories as antiquated and incorrect. He is, quite simply, wrong in all areas."

"Who's Zimmerman?" Jo asked.

"Someone who obviously ticked off Dr. Eve," Caylin whispered.

"He's a hack," Theresa responded. "Dr. Eve's research pretty much destroyed his theories. She's the real deal. She did her research in outer space. Zimmerman never set foot in an airplane. He hated to fly."

"I'm so glad you're here to tell us these things," Jo muttered, sinking into her seat.

"She's right," Santino said bitterly. "Zimmerman was an imbecile."

24

Dr. Eve continued her presentation, proving with a slide demonstration how Zimmerman's theories were worthless. Theresa was hypnotized, hanging on every word and nodding when she agreed with something Dr. Eve said. Which was pretty much everything.

Then a strange slide appeared on the screen behind Dr. Eve. The previous slides had displayed pie graphs and flowcharts, as well as photos of Dr. Eve working on the space station. But this one was different. It displayed a long, complex formula.

"What's that?" Theresa wondered.

"Uh-oh," Santino said.

Theresa noticed the twins sharing a panicked look.

Dr. Eve didn't spot it at first. She continued her lecture. Then she noticed the shift in the crowd. They, like Theresa, were all trying to decipher the meaning of the word *meggidion*, which was printed below the formula.

Dr. Eve whirled at the screen, then leveled a stare of pure rage at the twins. She barked a long, harsh phrase in Russian and dramatically pushed the handheld button that changed slides. The next one was another flowchart about her lecture.

Santino and Carlo sank into their seats, as if trying to melt away.

"I apologize, ladies and gentlemen," Dr. Eve said with an unhappy sigh. "If you'll allow me to continue . . ."

"What's wrong?" Jo whispered.

Santino smiled weakly. "Wrong slide."

"What's meggidion?" Theresa asked.

"It's a component of one of Dr. Eve's unsuccessful experiments," Santino replied. "It's rather embarrassing for her, you see."

Carlo punched Santino on the leg. "We are forbidden to talk about it, Santino."

Santino smiled again. "As my brother said." He gestured to the podium. "Please, the lecture continues."

The Spy Girls turned back to Dr. Eve. No other strange slides appeared, and the twins said nothing during the rest of the lecture.

When it was over, they all stood and stretched. "That was so cool," Theresa gushed. "Thanks for getting us in, guys."

Santino bowed. "Our pleasure."

"Well, we should get going," Caylin suggested.

"Wait," Santino said, holding up his hand. He turned to his brother and uttered something in Italian. Carlo smirked and nodded. "Would you like to meet Dr. Eve?"

Theresa's eyes bugged. "Are you kidding? I'd give my right arm."

"I dunno," Caylin replied. "We have something we

have to do. Something *important*, girls. Remember?"

"Come on," Theresa pleaded.

"It can't be tonight, anyway," Santino said. "Dr. Eve wants to get back to her château early. But tomorrow night she is hosting a reception for special guests of the symposium. Would you like to come as our guests?"

Jo smirked. "Guests?" she asked, implying she preferred the term "dates."

The twins grinned sheepishly at each other. Carlo muttered something in Italian. Santino laughed. "The . . . *appropriate* word would be guests."

Jo winked. "I get it." She turned to her partners. "What do you say, ladies?"

"We're there," Theresa declared. Caylin nodded.

"Fine," Santino said, his dark eyes glittering seductively. "Dr. Eve's château is the last house on Hauptstrasse, up on the mountain. Eight o'clock. And it is a formal affair. You will want to dress."

"Don't worry." Jo flashed a sexy little grin. "We will."

Someone barked a scathing order from the stage. They all turned and spotted Dr. Eve standing offstage, glaring at the twins.

"We have to go," Santino declared. "We will see you tomorrow night."

"Count on it," Theresa replied.

Santino yanked Carlo by the sleeve and they hightailed it up to the stage. Then they all disappeared behind a curtain.

The Spy Girls headed for the exit.

"I can't believe we're going to actually be at Dr. Eve's house!" Theresa said excitedly. "It's too cool."

"And the twins are too hot," Jo added. "Have you ever seen such sexy eyes?"

"Okay, guys," Caylin said. "How about a reality break? I think Carlo's hot as a pepper, too, okay? But we have a princess to find, and the clock's ticking."

"We have all day tomorrow to find her," Jo reassured her. "And hey, you never know. Dr. Eve is sort of A-list. Maybe Kristal will be at her bash."

"If you believe that, I have this white house in Washington to sell you cheap," Caylin replied.

They came out of the auditorium into the lobby. Dozens of people milled about, chatting up the lecture. Outside the massive front windows, the lights of Schnell Mountain made the snowy slopes glow.

"Man, it's not fair. We should just hit the slopes now," Jo said. She gestured at the crowd. "I mean, all these people can just slap on the skis whenever they—" Suddenly Jo paused, frozen in midpout.

"What?" Theresa asked.

Jo's eyes widened, and she frantically grabbed at the arms of the other two Spy Girls. "There, there, right over there," she whispered harshly, pointing.

"What?"

"It's Rook!"

et's get him!" Caylin ordered.

The trio plowed through the crowded lobby. But they weren't the only ones who spotted Rook. His dark looks and brilliant green eyes were legendary throughout the world. It was as if every person in Schnell descended on him at once.

Several burly bodyguards surrounded him and roughly plowed him forward, away from the surging crowd.

"They're heading for that nightclub!" Caylin warned. "We have to hurry!"

Theresa grunted, trying to push through the throng. "No way. It's not happening." She watched helplessly as the bouncers ushered Rook and his party around the velvet ropes and inside.

All at once the crowd dispersed. Jo sighed in disgust and straightened her hair. "If this is what it's going to be like whenever Rook comes into a room, we're going to have a very hard time with this mission."

"I say we go into the club," Caylin suggested.

"I am *not* dressed for that," Jo countered, brushing imaginary dust from her sweater sleeve. "I look like I just did a shift at a fast-food joint."

"None of us are dressed for it, Jo, let alone up for it," Theresa argued. "But Rook is in there right now. We've got him cornered. If we can get in there, it'll be dark. You might even manage to get past his bodyguards if you tease your hair a little."

"Thanks so much," Jo muttered. "Why don't we go back to the A-frame and do some serious preening? We'll get right in."

"There's no time," Caylin replied. "Rook could leave. And I don't think anyone has a better suggestion at this point. We have to try."

"Fine," Jo grumbled. "What a waste of a perfectly good nightlife."

"You'll live," Theresa said. "But you'd better turn on the charm because those guys look like they've heard it all."

Indeed, the four bouncers were megamen, each over six feet three and solid as brick walls in their heavy black turtleneck sweaters. As the Spy Girls approached, the lead bouncer's gaze focused on them from under deep eyebrows. His mouth curled into a smirk, and he folded his arms.

"Young Americans," he proclaimed in a thick German accent. "Looking for a good time, no?"

Jo turned up the wattage on her smile and stepped forward. "As a matter of fact, we are, Herr . . . ?"

"Dieter," he replied, his smirk growing.

"Dieter," Jo repeated, her eyelids fluttering seductively. "How sweet."

"Do her eyes just *do* that, or does she have to work at it?" Theresa whispered to Caylin.

"Shhh," Caylin said, nudging her.

"We couldn't very well visit Schnell and not grace Rik's with our presence," Jo continued, referring to the name of the club. "It is the fabulous place to be, is it not?"

"*Ja*, it is," Dieter replied with a chuckle. "But I must say *nein* to the young American girls."

Jo almost flinched. "*Nein?* Are you serious?"

"Perhaps the young American girls would like to come back when they are young American women," Dieter suggested. "Perhaps that would be better, *ja?*"

"*Ja?*" the trio repeated simultaneously.

Dieter leaned into them menacingly. "*Ja!*"

"Dieter, you're single-handedly setting international relations back about five years," Jo complained.

"*Sehr gut*. In five years you might be able to get into the club," he replied. "Until then you must go, fräulein babe chicks."

"Fräulein *what?*" Caylin growled, taking a step forward. "Could you repeat that, you Cro-Magnon excuse for a sexist pig?"

Dieter chuckled. "How threatening."

Theresa tugged on Caylin's sleeve. "Maybe it's time to go, girls."

"No, I want to know exactly what a *babe chick* is," Caylin retorted, fists balled tight.

"It's definitely time to go," Theresa demanded, stepping between Jo, Caylin, and Dieter. "We live to charm another day, okay? Say good night, Dieter."

"Good night, babe chicks," Dieter said, waving.

Once out in the cold night Caylin cut loose. "Can you believe him? *Babe chick! Babe chick!*"

"At least he was polite enough to call you fräulein," Theresa offered.

Caylin scowled. "Oh, save it."

"This is ridiculous," Jo commented. "I mean, look around." She gestured at the magnificent mountains all around them. The slopes glowing under their lights. The happy couples walking arm in arm to romantic dinners. The boisterous groups heading out for a night on the town. "We've got to get serious. Uncle Sam made this mission sound like a cakewalk, but it's going to take some serious spying. I don't know about you guys, but I want that extra week here."

"Me too," Caylin said glumly.

"We need some gear," Theresa stated. "Uncle Sam set us up with toys. We'll need the skis, but the snowmobiles and hot tub and big TV are useless. Even my computers can't help us much."

"What are you thinking?" Caylin asked.

Theresa smiled. "Let's get back and call the man. You'll see."

"So," Uncle Sam finally said, "that's all?"

Theresa chuckled. "How about a Cobra attack helicopter so Caylin doesn't have to use the ski lift?"

"Cool," Caylin chimed in. "I'll take it."

"Sorry," Uncle Sam chided good-naturedly. "I'm afraid not."

"Well, then I think this list ought to cover it," Theresa said.

"It's either this or you make us A-list movie stars overnight so we can crash any party in town," Jo added.

Uncle Sam's distorted image nodded and shifted from side to side in the large mirror above the fireplace. "That, Jo, I cannot do. You'll have the gear by morning. Plus you might even have a few surprises. However, I suggest you use the rest of your time wisely."

"If you would've supplied us with this stuff from the beginning," Jo said gruffly, "we might not have had to waste an entire night already. We'd be in that club talking to Rook as we speak."

"Easy, Jo," Caylin warned.

"She's just mad that her charms didn't work on Dieter," Theresa replied, smiling. "Her one-hundred-percent rate is down the drain."

Jo shot her an acidic look but said nothing.

"All right, Spy Girls, that's enough," Uncle Sam said. "You'll have your hardware soon. I'll expect a princess on my doorstep in two days. Good luck."

Uncle Sam disappeared, and the mirror reflected the room once again.

Jo sighed. "What a great mission."

"It'll get better when we have that gear," Theresa said. "We should have requested it before we did anything."

"Well, I don't know about you guys," Caylin said wearily, "but I'm taking a nice, long soak in the hot tub. Then I'm crashing. We've got slopes to hit tomorrow."

"You really think Kristal will be skiing tomorrow?" Theresa asked.

Jo nodded. "Every other picture of her in the *Tracker* is on skis. She'll be out there."

The Spy Girls nodded in agreement, but none of them felt very confident.

Jo opened the front door of the A-frame before seven the next morning. A large trunk stared back at her.

"Gear's here," she proclaimed.

Caylin looked over Jo's shoulder, her hot chocolate steaming in the cold air. "How do they do that? I didn't hear a thing last night."

"That's because you snore like an elephant," Jo replied.

"Elephants don't snore," Caylin replied icily. "And neither do I."

"Like an elephant," Jo repeated. "Ask T."

Caylin made a growling noise and grabbed a handle on the trunk. "Take an end."

Jo smiled and grabbed a handle. "My, my, aren't we touchy."

They hauled the trunk into the middle of the main room and popped the lid. Theresa joined them as they sifted through their equipment.

"Here's a standard cosmetic kit for all of us," she said, passing them out. "Includes lipstick camera, compact communications, and mascara."

"What's the mascara do?" Jo asked, opening hers.

"Just mascara," Theresa replied.

"And not even a very good brand." Jo sniffed.

"That's the government for you," Caylin replied.

"Here's an assortment of bugs and miniature video cameras," Theresa declared, "which would have been perfect last night for Rik's. If we can get one of these on Rook or his bodyguards, we'll always know where he is. And that means Kristal, too."

"What are these boots for?" Caylin asked, holding up a beautiful pair of winter hiking boots. "They're gorgeous."

"We didn't ask for them," Theresa replied.

"There's a note from Uncle Sam," Jo said, scanning a piece of paper. "Dear Spy Girls—Enjoy the boots. They're a bonus if you happen to have a princess sighting and no means of transportation. Simply click your heels and you're off. And let's hope you never have to use the belts. They are standard equipment for mountainous terrain. Just click open the buckle and pull. Regards, Uncle Sam."

Caylin clicked open a belt buckle and gave it a yank. A line of black mountain-climbing rope came out. "Whoa, cool! There must be a hundred feet in this little belt. How do they make this stuff?"

She pressed a button in the buckle, and the rope snaked back into the belt automatically.

"Let's check these out," Jo urged. She held a boot in each hand and firmly clicked their heels together. With a loud snap, two-foot lengths of ski erupted from each boot.

"Ski boots!" Jo cried. "These are so stylin'!"

"Great," Theresa muttered.

"What's your problem?" Jo asked. "We finally have some cool stuff we can actually use."

"Maybe *you* can."

Jo and Caylin glanced at each other. "What are you talking about, T.?" Caylin demanded.

Theresa looked away, setting her boots back in the trunk. "Nothing."

Jo leaned forward in anticipation. "Oh no. I don't think it's nothing. Not a chance."

"Lay off, Jo," Theresa warned.

"I agree with Flirty Spy," Caylin chimed in. "It's definitely not nothing. So talk, T. Or we'll request truth serum from Uncle Sam. And you *know* he'll have it here by lunch."

Theresa glowered at her cohorts. Her jaw worked back and forth, grinding.

But they still stared.

"Okay, okay." Theresa relented. "You were bound to find out anyway. I mean, we're in the Alps."

"What?"

"Spill it!"

Theresa's nostrils flared, her eyebrows quivered, her lips curled back in a snarl . . . and she said it:

"*I can't ski.*"

4

Caylin blinked. Jo's eyes bugged. Then they both giggled.

"T., don't take this the wrong way," Caylin said, holding her belly, "but you really, *really* need to get a life."

"Hey—," Theresa began.

"Really, T.," Jo added, "I mean, other than tail-gating, skiing is the single best sport for meeting guys! How can you have lived this long and missed out?" Jo's eyes turned dreamy. "The fluffy snow, the swoosh back and forth as you fly down the slope. Maybe the guy's in front of you, maybe he's behind you, but either way it's always better than flirting face-to-face. I mean, you get some hot ski pants, throw your hair back in the wind, add in the big boots, poles, and planks, and girl, you suddenly realize that you've never looked hotter. Trust me, Theresa, the lift line is better than any school dance I've ever been to."

Caylin snickered. "Oh, no no no, my dearest Josefina. You have it all wrong." Caylin jumped up on the coffee table and struck a surfer's pose. "A snowboard is the only true way to experience everything a slope has to offer. Take the balance and coordination you need to ski and multiply it by about six hundred thousand. Then you *might* be on the same planet as boarding. I mean, on a board you can literally *fly*."

Caylin leaped off the table, kicked out at an imaginary foe, and landed on the carpet without a sound. She turned to Theresa and smiled. "Meeting guys is just the gravy, T. The trip is the real trip, you know?"

"Whatever you say, ninjette," Jo scoffed.

Theresa sank back into the sofa. "I think we should just find Kristal. That's what I think."

Caylin flopped onto the sofa next to her. "And how do you propose to do that? Jo and I can hit the slopes. What can you do? Hack into the lift ticket computer to see if Kristal bought one today?"

Theresa's eyes narrowed in anger. "For your information, I have very specific plans today. I doubt you two have ever made a specific plan in your lives."

"What were you going to do?" Jo asked. "Not that your partners should know or anything."

"I signed up for a ski lesson," Theresa replied defiantly. "The school here says I can be up on the regular slopes by lunch."

Caylin laughed. "Up's the easy part. How did they say you'd be getting down?"

This sent Jo and Caylin into mad gales.

Theresa scowled. "Oh, come on! I mean, really! How hard can it be to ski?"

Theresa felt the world spin out from under her. Her heart shot into her throat, her belly lifted into the air, and her lungs deflated.

Then she hit the ground.

"*Oof!*"

"Still think skiing's easy, T.?" she heard Jo call out.

Theresa sat up. Her equipment was all around her. A ski. A glove. A pair of goggles. A pole, slightly bent.

How could she fall? She wasn't even going that fast. In fact, she was only a few yards from the A-frame.

"Are you in pain?" Caylin called from up the hill. "Pain's good. You should learn to like pain."

"You're sick, Cay," Jo replied, shoving off with her poles toward Theresa's crash site.

"Hey, I'm just trying to help," Caylin offered, slapping her snowboard against the slope and moving forward. "She needs it."

"I'm fine!" Theresa growled.

Jo cut her skis into the trail just in front of

Theresa as she stopped, spraying her with several pounds of snow.

"Sorry, I couldn't resist," Jo remarked, giggling.

"You two are the cruelest people I've ever met!" Theresa sputtered, brushing snow off her.

"Hey, what did I do?" Caylin said, sliding in next to Jo. "At least you learned the first rule of skiing."

"What's that?" Theresa asked.

"When in doubt," Jo replied, "fall."

"Thanks a lot."

"Can you make it to the lodge okay?" Caylin asked. "Seriously."

Theresa nodded gruffly, collecting her gear. "I'll make it. Even if I have to walk."

"Well, we have the communications and surveillance gear now," Jo commented. "Let's keep in touch. And find us a princess. What do you say?"

Jo put out a hand for Theresa. She grabbed it and stood up on her skis. Shakily.

Finally Theresa managed a smile. "I say okay."

"Good," Jo replied.

"Remember," Theresa said. "No matter what happens, we're still going to Dr. Eve's party tonight, yes?"

Jo grinned seductively. "I'd hate to disappoint the twins."

"Well, that's that, then," Theresa said, popping

off her skis. "I'm going for my lesson. I'll talk to you guys later."

"Hey, T.," Caylin called.

"What?"

Caylin grinned. "Break a leg!"

"I must look ridiculous," Theresa muttered as she trudged through the snow, approaching the lodge. She carried her skis and poles in a sloppy bear hug, stumbling every once in a while in her Frankenstein-like ski boots. She noticed several people pause to stare at her. "What's the matter? Haven't any of you ever seen an American before?"

Finally she made it to the ski school. Or at least to the sign that said Ski School Meets Here in several languages.

No one else was there.

Theresa sighed and dropped all of her gear in a heap. The skis and poles clattered, but she didn't care. Her arms were exhausted.

"That's no way to treat a brand-new pair of K2 skis," came a deep voice with a pronounced British accent.

Theresa turned, and when she saw him, she couldn't help it: She actually gulped.

The guy stood about six feet two. His hair was golden blond. His eyes dark brown. His cheeks were rosy from the cold, but his boyish smile said that the weather didn't bother him one bit.

"Here," he said, bending down and fetching her skis. "Like so."

He stuck them into the snow so they stood up to make an X. He stuck the poles next to them. "If you throw them around like that, you'll rough up your edges. Don't want that."

"Oh," Theresa replied, staring dumbly at him.

"Are you Tish, by any chance?" His eyes stared right into hers.

"Um . . . yeah," she stammered, looking away. "I mean, yes. I am." Why couldn't she talk?

"Perfect," he said, taking off his glove and extending his hand. "I'm Patrick. Your instructor."

"Oh," she said again. She blinked, felt horribly stupid, and then clumsily removed her own glove to shake his hand. His handshake was so warm and firm. The warmth seemed to course into her veins. "Nice to meet you."

"You've never skied before?" he presumed.

"No," she replied sheepishly. "Well . . . unless you count on the way over here. But I fell."

He chuckled. "That's all right. You should prepare yourself. You're going to fall quite a bit today."

Theresa returned the chuckle. "I can't wait."

She *still* couldn't talk! What in the world was she saying? Was she going to talk in one-syllable words all day?

"You're British, aren't you?" she managed.

"Yes, from London," Patrick replied. "I'm on leave from Oxford."

Theresa tried to keep her eyes from popping out of her head. A real, live Oxford man was teaching her to ski! Jo loved her diamonds. Caylin loved her workouts. But Theresa's magic words went strictly along the lines of Harvard, Stanford, MIT, Princeton, and of course, Oxford.

She actually had goose bumps.

"Is there much skiing in England?" she asked.

Patrick shook his head. "No. My family used to come to the Alps quite a bit when I was younger. I learned on these mountains. Now I teach here while on holiday." He grinned. "Are you ready, then?"

Theresa smiled nervously. "No, not really."

"Oh, relax," Patrick replied. "I haven't killed anyone. At least, not yet." He pulled her skis out of the snow and laid them side by side on the ground. "There you are. Step on in, and off you go."

Theresa stutter-stepped to her skis. She gingerly popped her skis onto her boots—the only part of the process that she really knew how to do.

"Wasn't that easy?" Patrick asked gently. "Didn't hurt a bit, did it?"

For the first time Theresa held his gaze. "I'm not six, you know."

He held up his hands. "Sorry."

"That's better." She couldn't help cracking a smile. "So what do you study at Oxford?"

"Archaeology, political science, and computers," he replied. "Not necessarily in that order, of course."

"Of course," she echoed.

"How about you?"

"I dabble a bit in computers myself," she said playfully, not mentioning the more colorful places she'd hacked into.

"Splendid," Patrick replied. "We'll have much to talk about." He gestured toward the beginner slope. "Shall we?"

Theresa's gaze followed the gentle slope all the way down to the distant chairlift at the bottom. It might as well have been Mount Everest. "Just like that? Don't I have to pass a written exam or something first?"

Patrick laughed. "Of course not. It's not so bad. You have to start with the basics. It's called the snowplow. You simply point your toes in, forming a triangle with your skis. Then you push out with your edges to slow yourself down. Like so."

He demonstrated, effortlessly moving ten yards down the hill as slow as a snail. But

Theresa had a tough time keeping her eyes off his muscular legs. The butterflies in her belly intensified.

"You want me to do *that?*" she asked, her fingers nervously flexing on her poles.

"I promise you won't get hurt," Patrick said, gesturing her forward. "All you have to do is remember one thing."

"What's that?"

"When in doubt, fall."

"I've heard that somewhere before," Theresa muttered.

Patrick waved her on. "No worries. Just point your tips toward me and push with your poles. Off you go, then."

Theresa drew in a deep breath . . . and pushed. She felt herself moving, picking up speed, faster, faster. Panic crept into her body, and she wanted to flail her arms. Patrick got closer and closer.

A low sound came out of her throat—something totally embarrassing that would be a full-fledged scream in two seconds.

Then Patrick was right there. She braced for a bone-crushing impact, but he simply hooked his arm around her waist and brought them both to a gentle halt.

"There, you see?" he said calmly. "You just skied."

Theresa smiled nervously. "Yeah, but if you weren't here, I'd be dead meat down in those pine trees."

Patrick gave her a playful wink. "Don't worry. If you got hurt, I wouldn't be able to live with myself."

She smiled, noticing how natural his arm felt around her waist. And how her heart sank when he took it away.

"Ready for your next challenge, Tish?"

She gripped her poles, smiled, and nodded. Maybe skiing wasn't so bad after all.

That night the Spy Girls took a taxi to Hauptstrasse and hoofed it up the driveway to Dr. Eve's château. Jo and Caylin complained the whole way that they hadn't seen hide nor beautiful blond hair of Kristal that day. She and Rook simply weren't making themselves public. The Spy Girls would have to take more drastic measures if they were going to—

Silence took over when the château came into view.

The trio just stood there and stared. And stared. And stared.

"Will you look at this place?" Jo marveled, breaking the silence.

Every window was lit from inside, casting a warm golden glow over the snow. The château seemed to be built into the mountain itself. It was designed in a definite alpine motif, with dark wood frames rising up to points all over the place. In many ways it was like a castle, but not made of stone. The front of the building was all windows, curving out over the hill to provide a breathtaking view of the valley below.

"Big bucks," Caylin whispered.

"See?" Theresa said. "Even science geeks can live like movie stars."

"You wish," Caylin replied.

"Well, even we'll manage to dress this joint up," Jo boasted. "As usual, girls, we all look fabu. One good thing you can say about The Tower: They know how to dress an agent."

The Spy Girls were decked out to the nines and tens—full-blown evening wear, cashmere overcoats, the works, even though the high heels were a little treacherous on the icy patches.

"The twins won't know what hit them," Jo said playfully.

"We're about to meet one of the most amazing women in the world," Theresa muttered, "and it still comes back to the boy toys."

"It always does, Theresa," Jo teased. "Speaking of which, do tell us more about your studly ski instructor."

Theresa felt her cheeks flush. "You've heard enough."

"Yeah, right," Caylin said. "You practically drooled all over your dress while we were getting ready. I think someone's got a crush."

"Cut it out," Theresa replied wearily. "He's an Oxford man. Your everyday, ordinary brainiac."

"Oooh, then T.'s *definitely* crushing big time," Jo chimed in. "But how did you find an Oxford man who knows how to ski? Shouldn't he be locked up in a computer lab somewhere, cleaning his screen?"

"Har-dee-har-har," Theresa retorted, even though she knew all too well that Patrick had never left her thoughts since she left him that afternoon. On their last run she'd actually made it all the way down the beginner slope without falling. Patrick had been so sweet, so patient, and so complimentary.

But the lift rides were the best part. That's when they talked about other things. Like Oxford. School in general. Computers. Dreams.

Patrick and Theresa were so alike. Caylin and Jo were right—she *did* have a crush on him. But unfortunately she had a mission to attend to. She couldn't spend every hour of the day getting ski lessons . . . could she?

"Do you really think there's a chance that Kristal will be at this party?" Caylin wondered.

"You never know," Theresa replied.

"There *are* a lot of limos in the driveway," Jo observed.

"Let's go find out," Caylin declared.

The trio reached the beautiful mahogany double front doors and rang. As they waited for an answer, Caylin stiffened.

"Do you see that?"

"What?"

"Up there, by that tree." Caylin nodded without being obvious. "Two men."

Indeed, two men clad in black leaned against a tree trunk several yards from the front door. The girls couldn't make out any other details.

"Relax, guys," Theresa said. "Dr. Eve has bodyguards. She's worked on a lot of big-time projects. Plus I'm sure her guest list is loaded with big names. Security is a must."

The front door swung inward, opened by a distinguished-looking man in a tuxedo. He said some curt words in German. *Guten abend* was not among them.

"Go ahead, Miss Science," Jo prodded. "This is your show."

Theresa stepped forward and smiled. "Hello. We were personally invited by Santino and Carlo. The twins. I'm sure everything's in order."

The man at the door said nothing. He didn't budge.

"Um, is there a problem?" Caylin asked. "Do you speak English?"

"I speak perfect English," the man replied. "Yet I react to what I do not see. And I do not see invitations."

"Yeah, but Santino and Carlo invited us last night," Jo replied. "You didn't see that, either, but it happened."

"Josef," came a voice. "Let them in." Santino—or Carlo—appeared over Josef's shoulder, smiling in his tux. "They are my guests."

Josef nodded stiffly and stepped aside. The twin immediately snatched up Jo's hand and kissed it. "You look positively radiant. Which is *molto pericoloso.* Very dangerous. You could melt the snow and cause an avalanche."

Definitely Santino.

Jo giggled. "That's the nicest thing anyone's ever said to me . . . *today.*"

Santino grinned. "Ah, touché."

The Spy Girls checked their coats and were escorted by Santino into the main living room—the front room with the floor-to-ceiling windows overlooking all of Schnell. Guests milled about, sipping champagne and sampling hors d'oeuvres. Everything was cocktail dresses and bow ties. Everyone was reserved and professional—as if they did cocktail parties for a living.

"I apologize for Carlo," Santino said. "He's indisposed at the moment. But he will be here shortly. Make yourselves comfortable, and feel free to mingle. Dr. Eve is looking forward to meeting you."

"She is?" Theresa asked, taken aback.

"Yes. I mentioned that Carlo and I had met three remarkable American women who follow her work closely. She was intrigued."

"Wow," Theresa replied. "Intrigued."

"Easy, girl," Jo joked.

"If you will excuse me, I must help with some of the preparations," Santino said. "I'll rejoin you in a few minutes."

"Take your time," Caylin replied casually.

"But not *too* much time," Jo added, smiling slyly.

Santino smiled back. "I promise."

As he disappeared, Caylin turned toward the food table. "Cool. Let's nosh."

Jo grabbed her arm. "Show some class, fräulein. This crowd eats their treats one at a time . . . *with a fork*."

"Give it a rest," Caylin scoffed. "They eat like everyone else. For free."

They pored over the food table, sampling everything. Jo scarfed caviar. Caylin stuck with shrimp. Theresa, however, just hovered, tapping her feet. Her gaze moved steadily across the room, in search of Dr. Eve. She couldn't believe she was going to actually meet her. This woman who had accomplished so much. Who knew so much and meant so much. This was truly a once-in-a-lifetime—

Theresa froze.

Her eyes locked on a figure across the room. But it wasn't Dr. Eve. It was Patrick!

He spotted her, too. He smiled and gave a small wave. The tux certainly suited him, no pun intended. To Theresa, he was a showstopper.

And like the first time she saw him, she gulped.

"You see a ghost, T.?" Caylin asked through a mouthful of shrimp.

Theresa didn't answer. She just kept staring at Patrick.

"No, Caylin," Jo replied. "She saw *that*."

All three Spy Girls locked eyes on Patrick, mouths agape. Caylin and Jo didn't realize it, but that meant their chewed food was showing.

"Who's that?" Jo demanded.

"Patrick," Theresa whispered.

"*That's* Patrick?" Jo said. "The geekly ski instructor from Oxford who likes laptops and fossils?"

"That's him," Theresa confirmed.

"I take back everything I said about you, T.," Jo gushed.

Theresa snatched a glass of champagne from a passing tray and stepped out. "See you guys later."

"I wonder," Caylin replied as Theresa approached Patrick. "Can you believe her, Jo?"

"Some girls have all the luck," Jo replied. "But remember, we have two hunky dates of our own. In fact, I think I'm going to go find Santino. He's neglecting his guest."

"Hey, what about me?"

"Carlo is lurking somewhere," Jo suggested, already on the move. "Plus there are a couple dozen shrimp left. Have a day."

"Thanks a lot."

"Be careful," Patrick warned. "That stuff goes right to your head."

Theresa shrugged. "I don't even know why I picked it up," she said nervously. "I don't drink."

She put the glass back on the same waiter's tray she had just plucked it from. The waiter rolled his eyes and moved on.

"If I may," Patrick said, "you look absolutely stunning."

Theresa blushed hard. "Thank you. So do you."

"I'm used to seeing you covered with snow."

"But I improved. You're a good teacher."

"You're a better student. You'll be on the big slopes in no time." He smiled. "If you decide to keep skiing, that is."

Theresa smiled back. "I'd like to. If you'd teach me."

Patrick cocked an eyebrow. "I'm not sure. I'm terribly in demand, you know."

"I'm sure," Theresa replied. "So what brings you to this party?"

"Naturally, I'm a fan of Dr. Eve's work in space. It's fascinating. When I saw that she was lecturing at the science symposium, I thanked my good fortune. As for the invitation, I sort of gleaned one from a rather wealthy dignitary who needed help with his slalom skills."

"I see," Theresa replied, spotting an opening. "So you must deal with a lot of wealthy people who want to learn to ski?"

"Some," he replied.

"Anyone famous?"

Patrick smirked. "Perhaps. Who did you have in mind?"

Theresa playfully made a circle on the carpet with her toe. "Well, I heard that Kristal is in town. And I'm a huge fan of her music."

Patrick chuckled. "No such luck, old girl. I'm afraid Kristal is the phantom of Schnell. Of course, the tabloids think she's here. But no one knows for sure where she'll pop up next."

Theresa sighed. "I guess I'm a little starstruck. I mean, meeting Dr. Eve is more than I dreamed of. I couldn't imagine meeting two of my idols in one week."

"You like the princess that much?" he asked.

Theresa nodded. "How can you not admire her? She has the perfect life. Anyone would die for that life." Sure, she was lying, but it was for a good cause. She *was* on a mission, after all.

Patrick nodded back. "I never thought of it that way."

Theresa hated deceiving Patrick. She wished she could tell him what she *really* thought—that Kristal was just a spoiled royal. But she had to find clues wherever she could. Patrick seemed to have the town wired. She figured maybe he knew someone or something. No such luck. And now he thought she actually adored the princess! She was making herself into a class-A dork in no time at all.

"If you'll excuse me, Tish," Patrick said. "Not to be indelicate, but I really must . . ."

Theresa smiled. "I think I get the picture."

"Right. Be back before you know it."

She watched him stride toward one of the back hallways. She let out an enormous sigh. Between finding Patrick, falling all over the slopes, meeting Dr. Eve, and trying to track down Kristal, Theresa couldn't believe she was still sane.

As the same waiter passed again she reached

out and snagged back her glass of champagne. This time the waiter stopped.

"Would you rather have the bottle?" he asked snidely, in a thick Russian accent.

Theresa chuckled lamely and returned the glass to the tray. "Guess not."

Jo slipped down a long hallway where there were no guests in sight. She'd glimpsed Santino going this way, but now he was nowhere to be seen.

She turned left, moved farther down the hall, and made another right.

"Don't get lost," she warned herself. "He's just a hunky Italian guy, after all."

She smiled to herself. "All the more reason to forge ahead."

She came to a spiral staircase. What to do? Up or down? She gazed up, but saw only darkness. There was light below and carpeting.

She went down.

She found herself in a den. The room was deserted. The furnishings were warm and luxurious. A fire roared in a fireplace even larger than the one they had in the A-frame. A huge stuffed elk's head hung over the mantel, its antlers reaching out like long, spindly fingers.

"Poor Rudolph," she whispered.

She spotted a doorway off to the right and went through it. A short hallway led to a closed door.

Light filtered through the cracks from beyond.

Should she open it?

"Well . . . you can always just say you're looking for the bathroom," she convinced herself.

She turned the knob, then paused.

Was Santino really worth getting caught over and totally embarrassing herself? Not to mention getting the Spy Girls kicked out of the only thing resembling an A-list party they could get invited to?

On the other hand . . . she *was* just looking for the bathroom. Right?

She pushed open the door.

She was at the top of another spiral staircase, overlooking a room that was considerably less charming than the den. There was a long conference table, a speaker-phone centerpiece, and a dozen chairs. The far wall was all blackboard. Totally clean. Portraits of other famous scientists lined the other walls. Einstein. Well, Einstein was the only one Jo recognized. She assumed they were scientists, but famous was a relative term.

She caught movement on the other side of the room.

Santino!

At least, she *thought* it was Santino. It could've been Carlo. Either way, that twin was hot in his tux!

He marched toward the blackboard wall, his back to Jo. She thought to call out to him, but waited.

Maybe she should sneak up on him and do a "guess who?"

The thought gave her shivers. Maybe he'd turn around and kiss her then and there!

She took a step down the spiral staircase.

Santino didn't hear her. He stopped at the blackboard and made a strange movement with his hand.

Jo's eyes bugged when an entire section of the blackboard turned inward.

Her inner compass told her that the blackboard wall faced into the mountain. Was there more to this château than met the eye?

Santino disappeared, and the blackboard slid back into place.

"How cool," Jo whispered.

She quickly descended the staircase and approached the blackboard. She ran her hands along the edges of the slate and its frame. There were no seams or switches or any other visible signs of a door.

It was totally hidden.

"This is *so* wild—"

Suddenly a series of loud pops came from the stairs. Jo's heart leaped into her throat. She gasped. She knew exactly what they were.

She'd heard those sounds before.

Gunshots!

"I'm outta here," Jo whispered.

Jo sprinted up the spiral stairs into the den. The place was still deserted, but the screams and chaos from the main room told her that she didn't want to be discovered here. There would be too much to explain. Even if it really *had* been a bathroom trip.

Adrenaline coursed through her as she marched down the hallway toward the party. She didn't have to worry about getting lost. All she had to do was follow the noise.

Suddenly a burly man dressed in black appeared before her. He held a semiautomatic pistol in front of him with both hands, battle ready.

She gasped, freezing in her tracks.

"Who are you?" he demanded, threatening to raise the gun.

"Don't shoot!" she squeaked, putting her hands up. "I'm just . . ."

Oh, what the heck, she thought.

". . . looking for the bathroom! Were those, like, gunshots?"

The man shoved past her. "Get back to main room. The party is over!"

He disappeared.

Jo sighed. What on earth had happened?

She found Theresa and Caylin in the main room. The guests were silently congregated in a tight group near the center of the room. Jo spotted Dr. Eve in the far corner. Several armed guards stood by her, their guns held loosely in their hands.

"What's going on?" Jo asked urgently.

Theresa shrugged. "We don't know. We were just standing here and some guns went off outside. The guards came rushing in and told us all to stay here."

"Who did the shooting?" Jo wondered.

"The guards," Caylin replied, her fists clenching anxiously. "I saw one of them pop in a new clip before."

"I didn't think the party would be this exciting," Jo said dryly. "You sure can pick 'em, T."

"Hey, I aim to please," she replied.

"Excuse me, everyone," came a voice.

The crowd turned. It was Dr. Eve.

"I wish to apologize for this outburst," she announced. "It seems to be a false alarm. But my security people feel it is best that we conclude this affair a little early. I am sorry for those of you who traveled so far to be here, but I assure you this is for the best. It seems my work has as many detractors as it does supporters. I am grateful to all of you, but unfortunately I must say good night."

The crowd dispersed. Drinks and food plates were set down. Low mutterings replaced the spirited conversations from mere moments before. Dr. Eve personally bid each guest farewell.

"Now's your chance to meet her, T.," Jo said.

"Great timing," Theresa replied. "Where are the twins to introduce us?"

"I don't know about Carlo," Jo commented, "but I found Santino downstairs. Before I could say anything to him, he disappeared through a secret door in a blackboard."

"Really?" Caylin said. "That's weird."

"Why is it weird?" Theresa argued. "Considering what just happened, you don't think Dr. Eve has to keep her work a secret? Of course she's going to have secret rooms."

"Whatever you say, T.," Caylin replied.

Then it was their turn to bid farewell to Dr. Eve. Jo and Caylin hung back, allowing Theresa to speak for them.

She cleared her throat, trying not to be nervous. But her words came out in one long blurted sentence: "Hello Dr. Eve my name's Tish I'm a big fan of your work and your accomplishments I think you're brilliant and your lecture last night was right on the mark. Basically."

Theresa paused, blinking, hoping she hadn't just made a fool of herself.

No one said anything for a moment. Dr. Eve stared at Theresa, taking it all in. Then, slowly, she saw Dr. Eve smile for the first time.

"Thank you," Dr. Eve replied. "I think."

"I—I'm sorry," Theresa stammered. "I'm a little nervous. You're, uh, one of my idols."

Dr. Eve looked at her thoughtfully. "Thank you . . . Tish, was it? I am a little nervous myself. I'm not used to gunplay outside my window."

"Um, me neither," Theresa replied.

Dr. Eve sighed. "The world is such a violent place. Too many people. Too much suffering. The pressure just builds and builds, and it needs to be released one way or the other." Dr. Eve smiled at Theresa again. "I'm glad you could come tonight, Tish."

"I'm sorry they—whoever—crashed your party," Theresa replied. "I was kind of hoping I'd get to talk to you tonight sometime. But I guess that idea's shot. Er, *gone*." She smiled sheepishly. "Sorry."

Dr. Eve chuckled. "You say you follow my work?"

"For a long time."

"Well, perhaps we can talk."

Theresa's eyes went wide. "We can?"

"I don't see why not. I have to make up for being such a careless hostess. I'm having some young students at my home the day after tomorrow. Perhaps I can give you a bit of a tour. In return, you can tell me your opinions on my work. I would be grateful."

Theresa's jaw dropped. "*You* would? Are you *kidding*?"

"I'll take that as an acceptance?"

"Absolutely. I'd be honored."

Dr. Eve nodded. "Very well. The day after tomorrow. Over lunch?"

"I'll be there," Theresa said, grinning from ear to ear. She shook Dr. Eve's hand vigorously.

"Good night, Tish and friends," Dr. Eve said, pulling away and waving. "I'm sorry it wasn't more of a pleasure."

Theresa waved as Jo and Caylin pushed her toward the door. They picked up their coats and followed the crowd outside.

"Wasn't that cool?" Theresa gushed. "I mean, as cool as there ever was cool?"

"What it is, is cold, T.," Jo complained, shivering in the frigid air. "We'll never get a taxi at this end of Hauptstrasse."

"We'll have to hoof it into town until we flag one," Caylin said.

"Great," Jo continued as they made their way

down the icy hill, slowly, in their heels. "What a great party. No dates, no fun, and nothing to show for nothing. Remind me why we listen to you again, Theresa?"

"You can't do it tonight, Jo," Theresa announced. "I'm a happy girl right now, and there's nothing you can do about it."

"I'm so glad you're happy," Jo muttered. "Your happiness, as always, is my happiness. Maybe when we get home and amputate our frostbitten toes, we can all be happy together!"

"You talk too much," Theresa retorted.

"And you—"

Jo was cut off by a cry from up the hill. Then a dark figure darted from the trees in front of them. It dashed across the road into the woods on the far side. Several guards pursued, flashlights bobbing.

"Halt!" one screamed.

The guard squeezed off a shot. The noise hit the Spy Girls all at once, like three invisible fists.

The guards flashed their lights into the trees, but it was too late. The figure was gone. The guards reluctantly retreated back onto Dr. Eve's property.

"There must have been an intruder," Caylin whispered.

"That shot scared the life out of me," Jo

replied, quivering. "I hate guns. They're so *loud*."

"Let's get out of here," Caylin urged.

"I'm with you," Jo said. "Theresa?"

Theresa didn't budge. She stared at the section of trees where the figure had disappeared.

"Hel-lo?" Jo prodded, waving her palm in front of Theresa's eyes. "Tower to Theresa. Do you copy?"

"What's wrong, T.?" Caylin asked. "You look like you've seen the proverbial ghost."

"I know him," Theresa replied, her voice distant.

"Who?"

"The intruder."

"You do?"

"Who is it?" Caylin demanded.

"It was him," Theresa said. "It was Patrick."

Back at the A-frame, Theresa and Jo lounged in their sweats, sipping hot chocolate. Caylin stoked the fireplace with fresh logs. Gradually the chill left them.

"What would Patrick want with Dr. Eve?" Theresa wondered aloud. "He's just a student."

"Who cares?" Jo remarked.

"I care," Theresa replied gruffly. "If he's trying to sabotage her work somehow, I owe it to her to find out as much as I can about him."

"I thought you were in love with him," Caylin said with a humorless chuckle.

Theresa smiled lamely. "That's the thing. I can't get him out of my mind."

Jo stood up angrily. "I've had it with this. Theresa, we have a mission, okay? And it has nothing to do with Dr. Eve, or Patrick, or the fate of humanity itself. It's a simple mission, one that I'm sure you remember. We have to find Kristal, and that's it."

"I seem to remember a certain Spy Girl falling all over herself to find a handsome young twin at the party tonight," Theresa replied bitterly. "And wasn't it you who suggested that Kristal might actually be at the party? I've heard some rationalizations before, but that's a whopper."

"We wouldn't have even *been* at the party if it wasn't for you, T.," Jo argued. "You just *had* to go to the lecture. You just *had* to meet Dr. Eve, your idol."

"We wouldn't even have gotten into the lecture in the first place if you weren't so obsessed with the twins!" Theresa fluttered her eyelids mockingly. "Oh, we have to meet them, oh, they're coming over, oh, how's my nail polish?"

"Yo!" Caylin interrupted.

Jo and Theresa fell silent.

"You're both out of line!" Caylin said, angrily tossing one last log on the fire. "We wasted an entire night on this party. And you're both to blame. Okay, we *all* are. No one twisted our arms, no one put a gun to our heads. Now we have less than thirty-six hours to locate Kristal and find some way to get her out of here. And I don't have to remind you that we don't have clue one where she is. I mean, we defuse bombs and steal secrets and prevent world wars. All of a sudden we're stumped?"

"I agree," came a familiar voice.

"Oh no," Jo muttered.

"Uncle Sam!" Theresa cried.

Their superior came into focus in the mirror above the fireplace. At least, as in focus as the computer distortions would allow.

"Caylin is right," Uncle Sam said grimly. "You've all behaved shamefully and unprofessionally."

"That's not fair," Jo argued. "This mission isn't exactly a world saver."

"That doesn't matter," Uncle Sam replied. "You are professionals, and you have been charged by The Tower to complete your mission according to the parameters set forth. It doesn't matter if you are recovering nuclear warheads or rescuing a cat from a tree."

Uncle Sam paused. When the Spy Girls didn't reply, he continued.

"Now listen carefully, ladies. Theresa, you will stop worrying about Dr. Eve's business. She has her own problems and her own people to take care of them. And if you need a ski lesson, ask Caylin."

Theresa didn't say anything. She just hugged a pillow and scowled.

"As for Jo and Caylin," Uncle Sam went on, "you will forget about meeting every handsome male on the slopes. You will focus on your mission, start looking for the princess, and stop acting like a bunch of giggling schoolchildren. That is the deal, and that is as good as it gets. Do you understand?"

Theresa stood up, tossed the pillow aside, and marched out of the room.

"I certainly hope Theresa is on board by morning, girls," Uncle Sam warned.

"She will be," Caylin said confidently, even though she felt anything but.

"Good. Because if you can't pull together as a team and finish this mission, you'll be of no use to The Tower. Do you know what that means?"

Jo and Caylin exchanged alarmed glances. "I can guess," Jo said.

"You'll be out of the spy business for good," Uncle Sam said.

The screen winked off, and the mirror became a mirror once again.

"I've heard *that* one before," Jo muttered.

Caylin flopped down onto the leather sofa. "Yeah, but I think he really means it this time."

Jo sighed. "Two strikes—"

"—and we're out. Game over. End of story."

6

Jo awoke with a start.

Someone had spoken to her. Or was it a dream? Her pillow was still there, the blankets were pulled up to her ears, and she still felt like sleeping for six more hours.

Everything was normal.

"Hey! Wake up!"

Except for Caylin shaking her.

"Go away," she replied grumpily.

"Wake up, Jo!" Caylin was already dressed in her ski pants and turtleneck. Showered, fed, and ready to kick butt. Jo hated her for it.

"Go run a triathlon or something," Jo growled. "I'm sleeping."

"Theresa's gone."

Now Jo's eyes were open.

"I'm dreaming, right?"

Caylin shook her head. "I just checked the whole place. Her jacket and skis are missing."

"I'm going to kill her!" Jo cried, sitting up. "What time is it?"

"Oh-seven-thirty," Caylin replied.

Jo bristled. "Do we need the oh? We're not marines. Just say seven-thirty, okay?"

"Don't take this out on me," Caylin warned. "Theresa's the jerk here."

Jo sighed. "What are we going to do? Should we look for her?"

"After what Uncle Sam said last night, I don't think we can afford to. She could be anywhere. We should forget about her and look for Kristal."

Jo nodded. "You're right. Give me a few minutes to join the living, and we'll jam." On her way to the doorway Jo stubbed her toe. *"Owww!"* she screamed, dancing on one foot. "Oooh, I'm gonna *kill* that girl!"

Caylin snorted. "Not if *I* get to her first."

Jo and Caylin surveyed the ski lodge from a table at the centrally-located cafe, sipping their hot chocolate.

"This is useless," Jo concluded. "We tried it before, and it doesn't work. Even if Rook or Kristal walked through here, we'd never get near them. We have to try something else."

"I'm open," Caylin replied. "But to what?"

Jo's eyes narrowed as a man strode by with a big camera around his neck.

"I think we should start thinking like the paparazzi," Jo said.

"How so?"

"Think about it, Cay. We've been issued some of the most advanced surveillance equipment known to humanity. Cameras, microphones, infrared, the works. Let's use 'em."

Caylin nodded. "Sounds juicy. But what good does all this stuff do us if we don't even know where to start?"

"I bet you a Swiss franc that we do."

Caylin laughed. "You're nuts."

"So you take the bet?"

"Sure, why not?"

"Pony up, ninja girl," Jo said, holding out her hand. "I'll show you."

Caylin fished a few coins out of her pocket and handed the cash to Jo, who stood. "I'll be right back!"

"Not if you're in a *Scream* sequel."

"Har, har."

A minute later Jo returned with a stack of newspapers. She dumped them on the table with a flourish. "Ta da! Welcome to the real world of journalism."

"You've got to be joking," Caylin scoffed. She picked up a copy of *Celebriteez* between thumb and index finger, as if it were contagious. "You want me to *read* this?"

"We're going to read them all," Jo said, flipping through the issues of *International*

Tracker, Infamous, and *Cheese!* she bought at the newsstand. "Whenever you see something on Kristal, tear it out. We'll make a pile. Any lead that mentions Schnell, we'll follow up. Easy, right?"

"Whatever you say," Caylin replied, opening *Celebriteez* and making a sick face. "Ugh! I can't *believe* the stuff they print in these rags!"

Jo flipped through the pages of *Cheese!* and laughed. "Hold your tongue, sister. Here's a story I *know* you're going to like." She tore out a photo of Kristal and Rook, accompanied by a short piece on a recent spat in a Schnell club.

"What club?" Caylin asked.

"Guess."

"Rik's?"

Jo nodded, flipping pages like a madwoman. She and Caylin continued through the whole stack, grimacing and groaning at some of the more ridiculous headlines:

OVERWEIGHT MAN STALKS BROADWAY
STAR—AND HE CAN'T EVEN WALK!

ALIENS BUY DELAWARE!

SHOCKER ROCKER SPOTTED BACKSTAGE AT DISCO
DIVA'S DEBUT—NAKED!

When they were done, they had a half dozen stories relating to Kristal and Schnell. Caylin slumped back in her chair. "I feel dirty," she muttered. "You actually like that stuff?"

"It's fun," Jo replied, picking up the first article. "And if it leads us to the princess, I expect you to subscribe."

"Over my dead body," Caylin retorted. "What's that one say?"

"Just that Kristal gave a quick concert at Rik's two weeks ago. She played a new song."

"Big whoop," Caylin replied. "What else do we have?"

"Kristal at Rik's, Kristal at Rik's, Kristal on the slopes, and Kristal—"

Jo paused, scanning the article hard.

"Well?" Caylin prodded.

A smile curled Jo's lips. She handed the piece to Caylin. "Read it and leap."

"'A source close to the royal family states that Princess Kristal and her longtime beau, Rook, have taken refuge in the honeymoon suite at the ultraexclusive, ultraswank Zürich Haus resort in beautiful Schnell. A spokesperson for the royal family in Zagaria flatly denies that Kristal and Rook have secretly wed and refuses to comment on the issue any further. Meanwhile, the happy couple has been spotted all over the trendy eateries and clubs of

Schnell.'" Caylin looked at Jo. "You don't think they're married already?"

Jo shrugged. "Who knows? But that paper came out today. It gives us a place to start. It says that the honeymoon suite at Zürich Haus is actually a luxury chalet out in the woods. If we could find it, maybe we'll find Kristal."

Caylin folded the paper. "It's a long shot."

Jo huffed. "We're running a girl short, we're in the doghouse with Uncle Sam, and we're getting our leads from tabloids. Everything we do from now on is a long shot. Let's go."

They bought a map of the town from the newsstand and located the resort, which was mostly a series of private, exclusive chalets in the woods. The honeymoon suite was the most remote one. Caylin scanned the ski lift map and pointed to one near the resort.

"I say we take this lift to the top, then ski down into the trees here. If we cut across the mountain, we should run right into the cabin from the back. Sound good?"

"It's our only choice," Jo replied. "We'll never get in the front gate."

They zipped up their coats, flipped out their ski passes, and marched to the lift they wanted. When it was their turn, they scooted into position and waited for their chair.

"Mademoiselles!" a French-sounding lift attendant cried. "You have no skis!"

Jo and Caylin glanced at each other and smiled. They simultaneously clicked their heels. Their ski boots snapped to life before the man's eyes.

"*Sacrebleu*," he whispered.

"Bye, now!" Jo waved.

The chair whisked them away.

It took Jo and Caylin two hours of trudging through two feet of snow, but they found it.

The chalet was tucked into a cul-de-sac at the end of a narrow road. It was a one-story little cabin with a carport, a hot tub, and an outdoor shack that appeared to be a sauna.

There were no signs of life.

They slipped in closer and saw the back end of a black sports car in the carport.

"It's a Lotus," Jo whispered. "Supposedly that's what Rook drives. Confidentially, I prefer the Lamborghini myself."

"You think they're home?"

Jo shrugged. "There's only one way to find out."

They edged closer to the chalet, slipping between trees. The snow masked their sound, but they knew they were hardly invisible. Hopefully no one would look out a window.

Finally they had their backs against the back wall of the cabin. There was a small open window a few feet above their heads.

"Use the camera," Jo suggested.

Caylin unlooped what looked like a five-foot section of vacuum cleaner cord out of an inside pocket. Yet it held its shape like a pipe cleaner. She plugged one end into a handheld mini-monitor and snaked the other end up the side of the building. It stood on its own, and in seconds the camera embedded in the other end was peeking in the open window. The picture on the LCD screen was perfect.

"The bathroom," Caylin whispered.

"I can see that," Jo remarked. "Zoom in on the shower door."

Caylin did.

"It's wet," Jo said. "And the mirror has some steam on it. Someone just showered. They probably have the window open to air out the steam."

"Bet you a Swiss franc that they're still home," Caylin replied.

"You lost that franc fair and square," Jo chided. "Okay. What do you want to do?"

Caylin thought it over. "Let's go in."

"We can't get in that window. It's too small."

"Let's go around. We'll find one. Or maybe a door's open."

"Ha! Nothing's that easy."

They circled the cabin, checking windows as they went. Every one was locked, every shade drawn. The only window without a curtain was the sliding glass door leading into the living room. They could see a dying fire in the fireplace, along with some room service trays with scraps of food and champagne glasses.

"Look out!" Caylin whispered, shoving Jo out of sight. "Someone's there."

"Who?"

Caylin shrugged. "All I saw was shaggy black hair and a bathrobe."

"Rook. That shaggy do is world famous."

"Don't you mean Scooby?"

"You're a riot, Cay. But I have an idea."

"Let's hear it."

Jo paused, glancing back the way they came. "I think I can fit in that bathroom window. Kind of drop in for a visit. What do you think?"

Caylin shook her head. "I think we're both totally postal. This will never work."

"Do you have any better suggestions?" Jo snapped.

"If we screw it up, Kristal and Rook will bolt. They'll dig a hole for themselves on some South Pacific beach, and we'll never find them."

"All the more reason to go in there now," Jo reasoned. "Because we *won't* screw it up."

"Okay, okay, let's go."

They retraced their steps. The window was about three feet above their heads and looked smaller than ever.

"A toothpick couldn't get in that window," Caylin grumbled. "And I'm sorry, but you're no toothpick."

"I beg your pardon!" Jo growled. "You just boost me up, blondie. I'll get in that window."

"I don't know if I can lift you," Caylin said.

"Oh, shut up."

Caylin snickered and made her hands into a stirrup. Jo put her boot in it and pushed up. Caylin let out an exaggerated groan.

"Shhh!" Jo scolded.

She reached up and grabbed the windowsill, pulling herself up to chin level. The screen lifted easily.

"I'm in," Jo whispered down to Caylin. "Give a push!"

Caylin shoved the bottoms of Jo's boots. Jo slid her arms inside, planted her hands against the wall, and pushed. The fabric of her ski jacket hissed against the window frame, but she slid in several inches.

"Harder!" she pleaded, trying not to make too much noise. "I'm almost in!"

Caylin heaved against Jo's legs and feet. She slid in farther, almost to her waist.

And stopped dead.

"What are you doing?" Jo cried. "Push!"

"I am!" came Caylin's strained reply.

Jo's eyes bugged. She tried to move any way she could—in, out, anything. Nothing happened.

Panic gripped her. She wiggled like a trapped worm.

"I'm stuck! I can't believe it! I'm actually stuck!"

She felt Caylin leap up and hang on her legs, trying to pull her out. It did no good. Caylin dropped off into the snow, and Jo hung there, arms and legs flailing.

"I'm gonna kill you, Caylin! Get me out of here! Do you hear me, you ESPN2-watching freak? I said—"

Jo stopped in midpanic.

A beautiful blond woman in a bathrobe stared at her from the bathroom doorway, jaw sagging. She was immediately joined by the man with the shaggy black hair.

The woman was not Kristal.

The man was not Rook.

All three stared at one another for a few seconds.

Then Jo smiled, waved, and said, "Hi!"

7

The sun set behind the Alps, throwing massive orange shadows across the snow. Theresa came skidding to a halt at the bottom of the slope. One of the big slopes.

Patrick slid in next to her.

"I can't believe I just skied down that mountain!" she gushed, her cheeks bright red from the cold. She slammed her poles into the snow happily.

"I told you so," Patrick replied. "Would I lie to you?"

Theresa laughed, but she truly wondered if Patrick really would lie to her. She took an awful risk blowing off Jo and Caylin. But she didn't care about the princess—not from day one. And Dr. Eve's work was important to her. To humankind. If Patrick was somehow trying to sabotage her, Theresa wanted to know. Now *that* was an important mission! Better than hounding a spoiled royal like a bunch of hyperactive groupies.

Unfortunately, her day with Patrick had been long on skiing and laughter but way short on answers. Every time she directed the conversation toward last night's party, Patrick steered it back to something else.

The truth was, Theresa didn't really mind. Even if Patrick was up to something sinister, spending the day with him had been wonderful. If there ever was a guy who spoke her language, Patrick was the man. And the fact that he was gorgeous didn't matter a bit—, yeah, *right!*

Still, Theresa knew she had to try one more time to get some scoop. It was her duty, after all. Sort of. In a lunatic-fringe-loner-acting-alone kind of way.

"I still can't believe you didn't hear any of the gunshots," she probed.

Patrick shrugged. "I guess that bathroom was on the far side of the château."

"How did you get out? I didn't see you."

"One of the security guards escorted me out. I walked down the hill and flagged a taxi. Though I have to admit, it was rather alarming stepping out of the loo to see a man pointing a gun at me."

Theresa laughed. "I bet."

Patrick cocked an eyebrow. "Why are you so curious?"

A slight wave of alarm passed through her. She had to be careful. Was she being too nosy? She smiled, shrugging shyly. "I don't know, Patrick. I was . . . well, worried about you."

Patrick grinned. "Were you?"

Theresa blushed. She couldn't believe she just said that! She nodded, feeling like a total dork.

"It was rather frightening," Patrick said, sliding closer on his skis. "I wish you would have been there to protect me."

Theresa giggled. "You are too smooth."

"And you are too beautiful."

She froze. She didn't know what to say. Her throat felt like one big knot. Patrick stared deep into her eyes, rooting her to the spot.

"Is something the matter?" he asked.

"N-no one's ever said that to me."

Patrick smiled, brushing a gloved finger along her cheek. "It's true."

Theresa's stomach did flip-flops. There weren't just a few butterflies in there. There was a swarm. She wanted to kiss Patrick so bad. But she couldn't . . . not if he was still a suspect.

There was so much about him she didn't know.

But he was so perfect. . . .

Then she had an idea. It might not have been

a brilliant idea, but it was the only thing she could think of. She had to know the truth about Patrick once and for all. And there was only one way to do that.

"I think you've got the wrong girl," she whispered.

He shook his head. "I've never met anyone like you, Tish. I know we've only been acquainted with each other for a short time, but you're definitely the right girl."

"Maybe, Patrick," she replied, pulling away. "Maybe I'm the right girl. But this is definitely the wrong time."

Patrick blinked, caught off guard. "Tish, I can't think of a better time. We've had a wonderful day. There's a beautiful sunset. We could have dinner, or—"

"No, Patrick. We did have a wonderful day. But let's not spoil it by pushing our luck." She reached out and touched his hand. "I have to go."

"Why?" he asked softly.

"I just do."

Theresa smiled, but she felt as though a fistful of daggers had slowly worked their way into her chest. She turned away—as gracefully as she could on skis—and pushed off. She didn't stop until she'd passed around the corner of the lodge.

Then she took a deep breath.

"I can't believe I just did that," she whispered, eyes shut tight. "I'd better be right."

She opened her eyes, turned around, and carefully peeked around the corner of the lodge from where she came.

Patrick stood where she left him, motionless. He stared toward the sunset. He looked so sad.

Theresa swallowed the lump in her throat, remembering her mission. "You had to do it," she told herself. "You *had* to."

After another minute Patrick lifted his poles and pushed off, heading away from her.

Now was her chance to meet the real Patrick. This plan was her only option, and she had to make it work. She just hoped she could keep up with him on skis.

Theresa gripped her poles and followed him.

"I can't believe you got stuck!" Caylin said with a giggle. "I would've given *anything* to see the expression on your face. But seeing your feet flailing like crazy was pretty good, too."

"I bet," Jo muttered, tossing a frozen-pizza crust onto her plate. "We're just lucky I popped out of that window when I did. The guy had the phone in his hand. I wouldn't want to have to explain that one to Uncle Sam."

"Think that guy called the cops?" Caylin wondered.

"Who cares. I've never skied so fast in my life."

"Fast? That was nothing. One time at Vail, I—"

Jo held up her hand. "I don't care, okay, Cay? I really don't. All I care about is the fact that we're a bunch of total morons, complete and unabridged. Theresa's AWOL, and we can't even infiltrate a honeymoon château without humiliating ourselves. I mean, what kind of spies are we?"

"We just had a bad day," Caylin reasoned. "Everyone has bad days."

"No, this trip has been a disaster since we got here. Uncle Sam is going to kill us. Or at least ship us to remedial spy school or something equally terrifying."

"You know, Miss Doomsday Device, we still have time."

"What's your plan? Break into the espresso bar and read bad poetry? We couldn't even do that without getting thrown in jail."

"Actually, I was thinking of taking on Dieter the bouncer again," Caylin suggested. "But this time we make it a little more fair for us fräulein babe chicks."

Jo's eyes narrowed. "What do you mean?"

Caylin grinned mischievously. "Come on. I'll show you."

* * *

"Now this is what I call using all resources at our disposal," Jo said naughtily.

She and Caylin entered the lodge and marched directly to the entrance of Rik's. A line of about twenty people waited behind the velvet ropes, looking hopeful.

"I think Dieter's about to have a heart attack," Caylin predicted.

"Oh yeah," Jo agreed. "Tonight we *own* this place."

The Spy Girl duo had changed tactics. They left the down jackets, ski pants, and clunky boots back at the A-frame. This time they raided the well-stocked closets for tight, slinky dresses, spiked heels, and full-length mirrors. Jo wore all red. Her black hair flowed around her face with a life of its own. Her face glowed with a paint job fit for a supermodel. Caylin chose a black spaghetti-string number, with her blond hair moussed, spritzed, and teased to the point of perfection. Lush, glitzy fake-fur wraps completed their ensembles.

When they neared the entrance, all eyes turned on them—the guys' opening wide, the girls' narrowing to slits.

They strode right to Dieter at the head of the line.

He grinned and held the velvet rope open for them. He gestured grandly with his hand.

"*Wilkommen zum* Rik's, fräuleins. *Haben Sie Spass!*"

Jo sniffed and brushed him aside. "Whatever!"

"Babe chicks coming through," Caylin announced.

Once inside, they basked in the moment, giggling madly.

"Oh, that was so choice," Jo gushed. "I'd give my top secret clearance to have that on video."

"It's pretty sad, if you ask me," Caylin said. "What was wrong with all those other people waiting in line?"

"They don't have government-issue Gucci," Jo replied. "Come on, let's take over."

They entered Rik's.

"Whoa," Caylin whispered. "Not bad."

House music thundered all around them from invisible woofers. Cocktail waitresses darted back and forth with full trays. The center of the place was the dance floor, packed with all the Euro—cool cats money could buy. They moved methodically, staring intensely into each other's eyes, but never smiling. Nine out of ten wore black.

The rest of the place was a maze of small tables and deep, dark booths.

"Do you see anyone?" Jo asked, squinting into the darkness.

"Someone definitely sees us," Caylin replied, gazing over at the main bar to their right. "Check it out."

"Why, hel-lo there," Jo said smartly.

The twins, Santino and Carlo, waved at them from two bar stools.

"Hello, ladies," Santino greeted, standing when the girls arrived. He kissed Jo's hand. "So nice to see you again. It's a shame our evening was cut short last night."

"It was a shame," Jo replied coolly. "I hope they caught whoever was responsible."

Carlo shot Santino a look. Santino smiled and said, "Yes, it was all taken care of. Perhaps you would like to dance?"

Jo's eyes lit up. "Indeed, we would."

"We would?" Caylin asked, shooting Jo a look of her own. "Don't we want to soak up the atmosphere a little first? You know, check out the *crowd?*"

Jo scowled and dragged Caylin toward the dance floor. "We can check out the atmosphere from the dance floor, can't we?"

So they danced, hopping and gyrating and flirting. Jo and Caylin indeed felt many eyes on them, but they didn't care. The music and the moment overtook them. By the time they made it back to their seats, an hour had passed.

"Whew, that was killer," Jo said, wiping her brow.

"You broke a sweat from that?" Caylin asked, barely winded. "You have to work out more."

"As if what you say will change the world," Jo muttered. She turned to Santino. "Do you guys hit the clubs often?"

"Yes, fairly often," he replied. "Our hours are long, so when we do get time off, we enjoy it."

"Do you see a lot of famous people in here?" Jo asked. "I mean, this is, like, the hottest club in the hottest ski resort in Europe. You must see a lot of glitterati."

"Some," Santino replied, his eyes darting from Jo's.

"Like who?"

Santino shrugged. "I don't know their names. I don't follow things like that."

"How about Tristan and Edith? Antonio and Lola? Colin and Vivica? Joel and Jane?" Jo asked, rapidly listing all the celebrity couples she could think of.

Santino stared stupidly. He obviously had no clue.

"How about Kristal and Rook?" Caylin asked.

That registered. Santino blinked and glanced at Carlo.

"No, no one like that," Santino said.

"Bummer," Jo replied. "We're big fans. We heard that she did some surprise concerts here. We hoped maybe we'd get lucky."

"No, I'm afraid not," Santino said curtly.

"Santino," came a voice. "It's time."

It was Carlo.

"You talk!" Jo said kiddingly.

Carlo gave her a dark stare. "Sometimes."

Santino caught his look. "I'm sorry, ladies. We must be going. We have an early morning tomorrow."

"So soon?" Jo moaned. "We were cooking out there."

"Again, I'm sorry. Perhaps another time?"

"Okay," Jo replied.

The twins dropped some money on the bar and disappeared into the crowd. Jo scowled.

"He didn't even kiss my hand good-bye," she said.

"Do we smell or something?" Caylin asked.

"Well, *you* do. I've been telling you that for weeks."

"Stand-up comedy is not your forte." Caylin said. "Maybe we should get out of here. Kristal's not going to show. She's—"

Jo poked Caylin in the ribs.

"Ow! What was *that* move?"

"Shhh!"

"You're shushing me in a hundred-decibel

nightclub? Did you have a thrombo or something?"

"Don't make a big deal out of it," Jo said, "but check out the guy in that dark booth over there in the corner and tell me we didn't just catch a big-budget break?"

Caylin peered into the smoky gloom. The man's face was illuminated by a tiny, dim lamp in the center of his table. Caylin saw shaggy dark hair, razor stubble, and shadowy, brilliant green eyes.

"It's Rook!" Caylin exclaimed.

"Shhh, if you freak out, he'll run," Jo warned.

"Where's his entourage?" Caylin wondered. "No security, no leeches, no nothing. He's all alone."

"He's all ours, you mean," Jo corrected, slipping off her stool and straightening her hair. "Turn on the charm, Spy Girl. We're going in."

They crossed the floor quickly, dodging dancers and waitresses. With each step they expected to be stopped by burly bodyguards. But Rook grew closer.

No one stopped them.

When they reached his booth, Jo slipped in on one side, Caylin on the other. Rook couldn't have escaped if he'd wanted to—and they both figured he'd definitely want to.

His tired eyes came to life when they edged in next to him.

"You're very cute when you're depressed," Jo commented.

"Oh, please, just go away," Rook grumbled, dismissing them with a wave. "Take your autograph-seeking, gold-digging selves as far away as those little spike heels will carry you."

"We don't want your autograph," Caylin replied, smiling at Jo.

"You want my blood, then?" Rook muttered. He rolled up his black sleeve and exposed his veins. "Take it. You're all a bunch of vampires."

"We don't want your blood, Mr., uh, Rook," Caylin said awkwardly. "We just want to talk."

"What my tongue-tied friend here is trying to say," Jo said, her flirtatious expertise taking over, "is that you looked very lonely all by yourself. You look like you could use some friendly company."

Rook snorted, knocking back the remaining liquor in his glass. "I have too many friends already. I don't need any more."

A waiter lurking in the shadows immediately set another drink in front of him, then disappeared.

"Good service here," Caylin mused.

"It pays to have roots," Rook replied caustically. "They know what I drink, how much I drink"—he paused to glare them—"and when I want to be left alone."

He gulped at his new glass.

"It seems to me that you don't have much to be unhappy about, Rook," Jo suggested. "You're rich, you're famous, and you've got one of the most beautiful women in the world to go home to."

Rook laughed bitterly. "You know it all, don't you? The *International Trasher* and all the others tell you everything there is to know about me, right? How much money I have. Where I'm spending it. Who I'm spending it on. Whether or not this weekend was the big weekend when I secretly got married. All of it. Am I right?"

Jo squirmed. "Not, like, totally."

"So, did you?" Caylin asked.

"Did I what?" Rook replied.

"Get married."

Rook laughed again and shook his head. He took another deep sip of his booze. "You certainly have the look down, I'll give you that. But you're too impatient."

"What are you talking about?" Jo asked.

"The two of you," Rook said. "You're beautiful. You've got someone buying very expensive clothes for you so you can get past a monster like Dieter. So you can get to me."

Jo caught Caylin's look: *Are we busted?*

"How much are they paying you?" Rook demanded, looking around. "Where's the hidden camera?"

"What are you talking about?" Jo asked again.

"You must think I'm stupid," Rook said. "You're reporters. Or you're stalkerazzi trying to get photos of me alone with two beautiful women." He raised his glass to the imaginary cameras. "Well, get a good shot. And for the benefit of your tape recorders, my official statement is, no, Kristal and I are not on our honeymoon. No, Kristal and I have not even been married. No, Kristal and I haven't spoken for days."

He downed the rest of his drink. The waiter in the shadows emerged with another. Rook snatched it from his hands and tossed him the empty.

He stood and raised the new drink. "Take heart, beautiful single women everywhere," he announced. "For alas, my beautiful princess has fled. I am alone. Kristal has left me!"

8

Jo grabbed Rook by the arm and forced him to sit down. If he made a scene, she and Caylin would be the ones kicked out, not Rook.

He slumped back into his seat, chuckling.

"We're not reporters," Jo stated.

"And we're not stalkers," Caylin added.

Rook's eyes narrowed. "Then who are you? You're too obvious to just be groupies."

"*That's* good to know," Caylin said, rolling her eyes.

"We . . . um, operatives," Jo said lamely.

"Operatives?" Rook mumbled.

"Covert operatives," Caylin said. "Our assignment is to find Kristal and return her home."

"Return her home," Rook echoed. "So you're secret agents?"

"Basically," Jo replied.

"And whose idea was this 'mission' of yours?"

Caylin paused before answering. "Queen Cascadia."

"Aarrgh!" Rook roared, pounding the table. "*I*

knew it! Her mother! She thinks she has such the iron fist. That monarchy is such a joke. But she must have gotten to Kristal. She must have!" Rook slouched in his seat and covered his face with his hands. "Unbelievable."

"Kristal just up and left you?" Jo asked, not quite believing it.

Rook leaned forward. His eyes were bloodshot. He looked totally defeated. "I guarantee it. You see, Kristal is very used to being loved. By everyone. She can't stand someone having a bad opinion of her, even is it's deserved. This is her way of calling it off. Just leaving me without a word." Rook snorted derisively. "All that cold royal blood, and she didn't even have the courage to dump me face-to-face."

"That's not an easy thing to do sometimes," Jo offered.

"Save the sentiment," Rook replied. "I need to be alone."

He motioned to the shadowy waiter. The man emerged and pulled the table away from the booth so Rook could escape. He was very drunk and nearly fell. Caylin grabbed his arm to steady him.

"Are you all right?" she asked gently.

His gaze met hers. His hard, bloodshot eyes softened slightly. "I'm destroyed."

Caylin helped him stand, then whispered in

his ear, "We're not the enemy, Rook. We're here to help. Can we contact you if we find out anything?"

Rook let out a deep sigh. He eyed Caylin suspiciously for a moment. Then he nodded. He told her the address of his château and what to say to the guards at the gate.

"Don't come near me before noon," Rook warned. "I will be hung over."

"Gotcha." Caylin stepped back. Several security guards/hangers-on had emerged from the shadows like the waiter. He really was never alone. They surrounded him, moved him forward, and disappeared into the crowd.

Caylin pulled Jo aside. "I have his address."

"Will you remember it?"

Caylin smiled and held up her handbag. "I activated one of my bugs. The whole conversation was recorded."

"Just like he thought," Jo stated.

"Oh, well."

"This doesn't make sense, Cay. He thinks the queen got to Kristal."

"If she did, we would have heard about it," Caylin replied. "Our mission would have been called off."

"You're right. I think this is worth a phone call."

* * *

"You're right, Spy Girls," Uncle Sam agreed from the A-frame's big mirror. "Queen Cascadia has had no contact with Kristal. I checked with her this evening. What does that tell you?"

"Maybe Rook knows more than he's saying," Jo offered.

"I don't know," Caylin said. "I'd say his broken heart performance tonight was pretty real. His whiskey breath sure was."

"Either way," Uncle Sam replied, "there's a big piece of this puzzle still missing. I want you to contact Rook again tomorrow—when he's sober. Check him out, check his place out, get a vibe. And Spy Girls?"

"Yes, Sammy?"

"Forget the three-day time limit. Just get the job done."

Jo couldn't contain her grin. "You got it! Not a problem!"

"As I said, *get the job done.*"

"We promise," Caylin replied.

"Good," Uncle Sam replied. "Now, Spy Girls, I have only one more question before I say good night."

"Let's have it, double-oh-Sammy," Jo chirped.

"Yeah, lay it on us," Caylin said.

The distorted image of Uncle Sam shifted, some of the pixels in his face turning an angry red. He crossed his arms, and they could feel his glare upon them.

"Where's Theresa?" he asked.

Theresa sat crouched inside a thick copse of evergreen trees, staring through her tube of Tower-issued breath spray that also happened to be a very powerful infrared telescope.

She was watching Patrick. She'd tailed him to one of the most remote ski lifts on the mountain and followed him up. The sun had just been setting, and while the view was like nothing she had ever seen, she noticed that the slopes below her got steeper and steeper. She didn't know where Patrick was going, but the trip down the mountain would be rough. And judging by the failing sunlight, dark.

However, once at the top Patrick took off to the left, into the trees. Wherever he was going, he wasn't taking the normal slope.

Theresa did her best to follow, ducking under tree limbs and using her poles to keep from falling into the deep powder.

She failed several times, eating her share of flakes.

Luckily Patrick took his time. She ended up falling one last time into her current hiding place, brushing herself off, and spotting the dark shape of Patrick a few dozen yards away.

"Okay, dream boat," she whispered. "What's your deal?"

She popped the cap on her zoom lens and zeroed in on him.

He was studying several large steel vents that seemed to grow out of the mountainside. The snow had melted around the vents, exposing the ground.

"What's that all about?" Theresa wondered. She clicked the record button on the telescope and captured the moment for posterity.

Theresa scanned the mountainside for more vents, but saw nothing.

Hmmm . . .

She capped her spy gear, grabbed her poles, and pushed off toward Patrick. If she could get closer, maybe she could see more. Her little telescope was only so powerful.

If she could just stay quiet enough to—

Theresa's left ski hit a patch of ice beneath the powder. She lost control of that entire side of her body, pitching wildly. Her poles flailed, and it was all she could do not to scream her head off.

She picked up speed, faster and faster. Trees whipped by her, branches stung her face, and she burst out of some evergreen branches to see Patrick. Faster than light and larger than life.

Bam!

They went down in a hail of equipment. Poles flew, goggles spun, and limbs tangled.

When they came to a stop, Theresa found herself on top of Patrick, staring right into his wide eyes.

"Uh, hi."

Patrick blinked. "Tish?"

"In the flesh." She shrugged. "And snow."

He shoved her off and rolled away. "Are you mad? What are you doing here? You could get us both killed!"

"My skiing's a lot better," she replied. "Killing us is a little extreme, don't you think?"

"That's not what I—" Patrick sighed and gathered up her equipment. "Look, just get your skis back on. I'll make sure you get to the bottom of the hill safely."

Theresa didn't budge. "What are you doing up here, Patrick?"

Patrick glared. "I could very well ask you the same thing."

"I followed you," Theresa replied defiantly.

"Why? I thought you made it painfully clear that you didn't want to see me again."

"I did?"

"You most certainly did!"

Theresa shrugged. "I guess you're just irresistible, Patrick."

"Not bloody likely." His eyes narrowed, and

he took a step forward. "A girl who can't ski doesn't follow someone to the most remote part of the mountain without a good reason."

Theresa grabbed her orphan ski from him. "The other person must have a pretty good reason for going to the most remote part of the mountain in the first place."

Patrick popped his own skis back on and hefted his poles. "Don't you suppose that's none of your business?"

"Maybe." Theresa nodded as she clicked her ski on. "The same way these big vents are none of *your* business."

"You really shouldn't be here, Tish."

"Neither should you."

Patrick scowled. "You don't understand. If we get—"

"*Hey!*" came a gruff voice from up the hill.

"—caught?" Theresa finished for him.

"Yes," Patrick replied. "Caught was *definitely* the word I was searching for!"

Who is that up there?" Theresa whispered.

Two figures emerged from the trees above the vents. Both were on skis. But neither of them had poles.

They had submachine guns.

"Uh-oh," Theresa moaned.

Patrick slowly pulled his goggles down over his eyes. He clicked a button on the side, and Theresa swore they came to life. They hummed, and a dim green light glowed from inside them. She'd seen that before.

Night vision.

The armed skiers closed in.

"Tish?"

"Yes, Patrick?" she whispered nervously.

"You're about to get the skiing lesson of your life."

He shoved her down the hill. Theresa screamed and almost fell immediately, but regained her balance enough to see Patrick pass her. He was crouched in a downhiller's pose, poles back, head down. Full speed ahead.

"*Stop!*" came a voice from behind them.

A gunshot rang out.

"Oh man, no guns! No guns!" she cried.

She didn't look back. She didn't stop. She couldn't have if she wanted to.

All Theresa could do was point her skis downhill, follow Patrick, and pray.

The wind whipped her face. She hadn't had time to retrieve her own goggles, and now her eyes watered badly in the cold. In seconds she could barely see. She wiped at her face with her glove, but it didn't help.

Panic gripped her.

A tree shot by. Her right ski grazed it.

Another shot rang out somewhere behind her.

Up ahead, Patrick was gone.

"Oh no."

She was a goner for sure. But she couldn't stop. The gunmen would catch her and kill her. How did she get herself into these things?

Another tree raced by, too close. If she hit one of them at this speed . . .

Then she remembered: the first rule of skiing.

When in doubt, fall.

But she was going too fast!

What was worse, getting shot or slamming into a tree? Equally bad, she thought. Both options would leave her dead. And falling? How about a broken neck?

A third shot rang out.

Theresa yelped—the slug took a chunk out of a tree just in front of her. Bark sprayed her as she passed.

"Patrick!" she screamed.

He seemed to emerge from the trees themselves. It was actually him. He was skiing next to her, a reassuring hand on her arm. Where did he—?

"Steady!" he called. "Grab my waist!"

He pushed just ahead of her. His movements were smooth and calculated. In a split second he'd stepped in front of her. She grabbed his waist, trying not to lose her balance. If she did, they'd both buy it.

Patrick guided Theresa through trees, over moguls that nearly threw them both in the air, and down a mountain that Theresa couldn't have skied alone without serious injury. Patrick made her feel as if she could do anything.

Several more shots rang out.

Something whizzed over Theresa's head.

"That was too close!" she called.

"We need speed!" he yelled back.

He suddenly crouched in front of her and slowed down. *Slowed down?*

"Patrick, what are you—*whoaaa!*"

When he slowed, Theresa bumped into him, almost flipping right over his head. Just then he stood up sharply on his skis. Theresa felt her body lift with his. Her skis left the snow.

She was riding him piggyback.

"Hang on, old girl!" he said.

"Don't caaaall me thaaat!"

Their speed rocketed. Theresa wanted to close her eyes, but she just couldn't. She had to see.

More shots exploded behind them. But Theresa swore they were more distant. No bark exploded in their faces.

"Hope you're bullet-proof!"

"Shut up and ski, you idiot!"

He did. Theresa chanced a glance behind them, but the trees were a blur. She spotted something far to her right, up the hill. Lights. Glass. A house. It looked familiar.

Dr. Eve's château!

They were that close?

Just then they hit a massive mogul. Theresa's stomach lurched. She felt weightless.

They were airborne.

The world went super slo-mo.

This was it. They would land. Fall. Break legs. Get caught. Be shot. Every fear pumped through her. All Theresa could do was grip Patrick tighter.

When they hit, she felt the air rush out of him. His legs buckled. Snow sprayed up into her face, blinding her. But the wind kept whipping her. Their speed didn't waver.

They didn't fall!

Theresa howled in triumph and hugged Patrick. They soared into a thick stand of evergreens. The branches reached out at them, snapping and yanking their clothes. But nothing could stop them now.

They burst through the trees. Just below them twinkled the lights of the town.

Theresa looked over her shoulder. All she saw were trees and the trail of Patrick's skis.

"We made it!"

They finally stopped just outside of town, in the shadow of a hundred-foot fir tree. They were invisible from the road. Patrick collapsed in the snow. Theresa landed on top of him.

"My bloody legs are on fire," he muttered. "How much do you weigh?"

"Didn't anyone tell you that it's not polite to ask a girl her weight?"

"Why don't you get off me and I'll consider it."

Theresa rolled off Patrick and stood uncertainly. Her own legs felt like butter. There had to be more adrenaline in her veins than blood. She couldn't stop her hands from shaking.

Patrick rolled over and massaged his legs. "Are

you all right?" he asked, huffing. "No bullet holes?"

"I'm okay. But who *were* those guys?"

Patrick chuckled. "Ski patrol. We were undoubtedly in a restricted area."

"Very funny. What were you doing up there, Patrick?"

"Seeking new downhill challenges," he replied smoothly. "The expert slopes are dead boring. Don't you think?"

"I think I'd like to turn next time I go down a slope."

"Well, I know one thing," Patrick offered, standing up.

"What?"

"I'm one fantastic ski instructor. You were great."

Theresa laughed. "Not great. Just alive."

Patrick nodded. "I think we'd better get moving. Who knows what will come down that mountain after us. Do you think you can make it on your own?"

A pang of alarm went through her. Not because she couldn't make it home alone, but because she didn't want Patrick to leave. She felt electrified after their ordeal. She just wanted to kiss him silly.

"Um, I guess I'll be all right," she said.

"Tish, I think . . . I think it's best that we don't

think too much about what just happened. Okay?"

"Yeah, *right*," she replied. "I'm not shot at every day. Something serious is going on, Patrick, and I think you owe me an explanation."

"Tish," Patrick replied, a pained look on his face. "It's really best that you don't know."

"That's not fair!" she cried. She bent down and retrieved one of her ski poles. "We just—"

When she turned back, she froze.

Patrick was gone.

"Patrick?" she called.

No answer. Just a silent, snowy night. He had completely disappeared.

Theresa sighed. "No fair."

Theresa skied back to the A-frame, thinking back on her exciting night. It had been like no other. Usually girls her age were thrilled just to be able to go to the prom with their boyfriends. But tonight Theresa had followed the man of her dreams up a mountain and skied down with him while being shot at.

"Not bad, Spy Girl," she whispered to herself as she locked her skis in the ski rack. "Not bad."

Still, she knew there were too many unanswered questions. Questions she couldn't ignore.

She clomped into the A-frame with her ski boots still on. She didn't even get a chance to close the door.

"Nice to see you, Theresa," Caylin said, arms folded, foot tapping.

"Where have you been, young lady?" Jo demanded, not a hint of humor in her voice.

"Let me guess," Theresa replied wearily. "You were worried sick."

"You wish," Jo said. "But Uncle Sam was *very* interested in your whereabouts. I'm never lying for you again."

Theresa glared back at her. "I never asked you to lie in the first place."

"What's the story?" Caylin asked angrily. "You owe us an explanation, Theresa. You let us down today."

Theresa sighed and bent stiffly to unbuckle her boots. "You wouldn't believe me if I told you. I'm dying for a hot bath."

"Try us," Jo ordered.

"I decided to continue my investigation of Patrick. Something is definitely up with him and Dr. Eve. I owe it to her to find out what."

"You *owe* it to her?" Jo asked incredulously. "Are you serious? You don't even know her!"

"I know her work, Jo. It's more important than rescuing any princess. I mean, what are we, a bunch of Luke Skywalkers?"

"It doesn't matter what you think of the mission," Caylin reminded her. "You're not supposed to think about it. Just do it."

"Shoe commercial sentiments from the jock," Theresa muttered. "How quaint."

Caylin took a step forward, but Jo put up her hand. "So what is it, T.? Really. Are you in love with this guy, or what?"

Theresa shot Jo a withering look. "Dr. Eve's mission in life is to help humanity, Jo. And she has the power and knowledge to actually do it. As a student of science—and a human being—how can I stand by and watch someone try to hurt her? How?"

"Uncle Sam said it himself: Dr. Eve has her own people to handle that," Caylin explained. "You were ordered to back off."

"Yeah, back off and chase Kristal, I know." Theresa angrily tossed her ski boots in the corner. "Real humanitarian aid. Well, I'm not doing it."

Jo blinked. "What did you say?"

"You heard me."

"No way," Caylin argued. "You're helping us with Rook tomorrow."

"You finally found him?" Theresa asked.

"No thanks to you," Jo replied. She quickly explained their encounter with Rook in the nightclub, along with Uncle Sam's orders to contact him the next day.

"I'm happy for you guys," Theresa said. "But I'm still not going. Dr. Eve invited me to her château, remember? I'm not passing that up."

"You're playing with all our lives, T.," Caylin warned. "If we fail, we're through. Do you understand that?"

"I'm sorry, Cay. But I think helping a Nobel Prize winner continue her work safely is more important than returning a spoiled royal to her mother, who was once a spoiled royal herself."

"You're forgetting something," Jo said.

"What?"

"You're a Spy Girl. Like it or not, you're part of a team. And this team has a mission."

Theresa shook her head. "That mission isn't for spies. It's for baby-sitters. I'm the one with the real mission. So you know what that makes me?"

"What?" Caylin asked.

"The *real* Spy Girl."

At noon the next day Theresa took a taxi to the end of Hauptstrasse and walked up the long driveway to Dr. Eve's château. The whole time all she could think about was the previous night.

She didn't know what would happen with the Spy Girls. She left before they were awake and ate a long breakfast at the lodge. No matter how many times she ran it back in her head, she still couldn't bring herself to work on the Kristal case while she could help Dr. Eve. It went against everything she stood for.

So many questions . . .

She was sure that the gunman the night of Dr. Eve's party had been Patrick. But what was he doing near those vents? And what were the vents for?

They'd skied right past Dr. Eve's château last night. That couldn't have been a coincidence. And Patrick had been too well prepared. No one skied with night-vision goggles.

Nothing added up.

She approached the beautiful mahogany double doors of Dr. Eve's château and rang the bell. She saw no armed guards. Nothing unusual. The butler answered the door and showed her in immediately.

Theresa entered the main living area. It was even more spectacular during the day. Outside the windows were miles and miles of snow-capped mountains and evergreen forest. The natural light in the room was almost blinding.

Dr. Eve was there, too. A cluster of students Theresa's age surrounded her. Special guests from the science symposium, no doubt.

Dr. Eve strode over as soon as she saw her.

"Tish, so wonderful of you to come!"

Theresa shook Dr. Eve's hand, and all of her worries instantly disappeared.

Jo and Caylin rode the Snownuke 667 over to Rook's place. Actually, Jo drove. Caylin held on for dear life.

"This isn't funny anymore!" she cried as Jo nearly sideswiped yet another car. "We're not supposed to ride this thing in the middle of town!"

"Relax," Jo muttered. "You act like I've never done this before."

Jo blew through town and across an open field to get to Rook's. While crossing the field, Caylin got a glimpse of the speedometer: 105! Wait—that was kilometers. But still . . .

She closed her eyes and prayed.

Finally Jo slowed down as they entered the posh neighborhood where Rook hung his hat. And these days, his head.

They found his house without a problem. It was gorgeous. A sprawling mansion behind a tall stone wall. There was an intercom at the front gate.

Jo buzzed it.

"What?" a gruff voice demanded.

Jo said the password that Rook had given them the night before and told the voice that they were there to see him.

There was a moment of silence on the other end.

Then the gates creaked open.

Jo drove the sled up the snow-covered driveway and parked it next to Rook's black Lotus.

"Wow," Jo marveled, running her hand over the Lotus's hood. "What a sweet ride."

"Come on, speed demoness," Caylin urged.

The front door was open a few inches. A thunderous techno riff roared out at them. They pushed the door open wide and went in.

Immediately they were hit with the smell.

"Oh, man, there is definitely a bachelor in the house," Jo grunted, wincing.

"It's like cigarettes, body odor, and really old socks mixed together," Caylin added.

Indeed, the house would have been beautiful under normal circumstances. But Rook was obviously living very alone, no matter how many hangers-on he had. Take-out food cartons, dirty clothes, and torn newspapers littered the living room. Beyond that was a den with a cathedral ceiling. A massive stereo pumped the music through speakers as tall as the Spy Girls. The tune echoed off the high ceiling, making them feel as if they were in a concert hall.

Rook padded out of the kitchen in a wrinkled muscle shirt and pajama bottoms. He held a cup of black coffee. His eyes were even redder than they'd been the previous night. Medusa would have been envious of his hair.

"I guess I wasn't dreaming last night," he muttered, sipping the coffee. "You were real."

"Yeah!" Jo hollered over the music. "Can you turn that down? We can't hear you!"

Rook nodded and pointed a remote at the stereo. The sound receded.

"Doesn't that hurt your head?" Caylin asked.

Rook chuckled. "Not that song."

"Why not?"

124

He sighed, stepped down into the den area, and slumped into an easy chair. He didn't offer them anything, and he didn't ask them to sit.

So they sat, anyway.

"It's the last song I ever heard Kristal sing before she left," he explained. "She sang it to me."

"When was the last time you saw her?" Jo asked.

"The night she left me, obviously," Rook replied bitterly.

"What happened?"

Rook rubbed his eyes. "We were at Rik's. Partying hard, like usual. Then some noisy fans demanded that Kris get up and sing. She felt like it, so she did. The last song she sang was this one." He gestured at the stereo. "It's called 'Eve of Destruction.' She's going to release it as the first single off her new album. Anyway, she sang the song. She stared at me the whole time. I mean, you know how that girl is famous for her blue eyes. We've been together for years . . . and those eyes still melt me, you know? She had me in the palm of her hand while she sang that song. And she knew it. When she finished, she smiled at me from the stage. Then she walked backstage. And I haven't seen her since. She walked right out on me." He chuckled angrily. "Sometimes I still can't believe it."

The song ended. The tape recycled and began again.

"Is that a demo tape?" Caylin asked.

Rook nodded. "It's the only copy I have. I don't know if I'll have the heart to buy the CD when it's released next month."

Caylin stood and approached the stereo. Jo ignored her, concentrating on Rook.

"Why would she leave you, Rook? Everything I've read says you two were happy. Total Cinderella factor."

Rook scoffed. "Everything you read, huh? Well, we *were* happy. I guess that makes me Cinderfella. The only time we ever fought was when the press got too close. Or when her family stuck its royal nose where it didn't belong. They must have finally gotten to her."

I don't think so, Jo thought. And that was right from the queen's mouth.

"I need more coffee," Rook said. He got up and shuffled to the kitchen, swinging the door behind him.

"What do you think?" Jo asked Caylin.

"Shhh," Caylin replied. "Listen to this."

She upped the volume on the stereo. Jo really tuned in to the song for the first time.

Her eyes widened.

Caylin saw the reaction and nodded urgently. "Do you hear what I hear?"

"Affirmative, Sporty Spy," Jo said breathlessly. "Could it be true?"

"There's one way to find out."

Rook came back in with fresh coffee. He didn't look any better.

"Rook, what's the story behind this song?" Caylin asked.

Rook stared blankly. "The story?"

"What does it mean?" Jo clarified. "What was Kristal talking about when she wrote it?"

He shrugged. "She's gone gonzo for this environmental stuff. She said something about donating all the proceeds from this song to enviro-warriors or something. I can't always keep track of what's in her head most times. I just love the song."

"Do you have a lyric sheet?" Jo asked.

"Nope. Don't need one. I know this tune by heart. Want me to sing it?"

"No thanks," Caylin declined. "But could you write it out for us?"

"You think it'll help?"

Jo and Caylin glanced at each other.

"*Totally*," they said in unison.

Rook found some paper and scribbled out the lyrics. He handed it over to the girls with a bewildered look on his face.

Caylin read the chorus aloud: "'She'll find what she's looking for/Find the key to a worldwide door/She'll open it up and spread the gloom/

Unleash the poison that seals your doom. . . .'"

Caylin paused, but Jo gestured for her to continue.

"'Call it pain/Call it knowledge/Call it rain/Call it college/It's the world gone bad/It'll make you sad/It's a global reduction/Called the eve of destruction. . . .'"

"Kris kept talking about poison when she wrote that," Rook said. "You know, how the world is being choked off. Stuff like that."

"I think Kristal's talking about someone specific," Caylin said, her face pale.

"What?" Rook asked.

"Her name is Eve," Jo said grimly. "Eve of Destruction. But you can call her *Doctor* Eve."

"I'm glad you decided to stay behind after the main tour, Tish," Dr. Eve said. "You show a lot of enthusiasm and promise."

"I hope so," Theresa replied. "Your lab is amazing. You actually built it into the side of the mountain. I've never seen anything like it."

It truly *was* amazing. After lunch the other students departed. But Dr. Eve had invited Theresa to stay behind. She offered to show her the real laboratory. The one on the tour was just for demonstrations.

Theresa was so excited at the offer that she only nodded over and over. She didn't want to open her mouth and sound like a dweeb.

Dr. Eve led her downstairs and through several rooms, one of which looked like a hunter's trophy room. A massive elk's head hung over the fireplace. Soon they were in the large conference room that was part of the original tour. Dr. Eve approached the blackboard and touched the frame.

An entire section of the wall opened inward!

Theresa's eyes bugged. "Whoa!"

Dr. Eve showed her many things. Some of her current work on the long-term side effects of weightlessness. Space colonization theories. And her crowning achievement: water purification.

"I study space for population purposes," Dr. Eve explained. "We will have to live in space eventually, for there will be no room for us down here. And I study water for the subsequent pollution that accompanies population growth. If we do not have pure water, we will die."

Dr. Eve led her through several chambers, each relating in some way to her research. Several lab techs milled about, ignoring them.

Theresa walked by a ventilation grate and felt a cold breeze hit her face. That was strange. Where would cold air be coming from?

She recalled the large vents on the mountain. Was this what Patrick was looking for? An entrance to Dr. Eve's lab?

Dr. Eve's head whipped around. "What are you looking at, Tish?"

Jo and Caylin raced back to the A-frame on the Snownuke. Jo pushed it even faster than before, forcing Caylin to hold on tight. She screamed into Jo's ear as they went.

"I hate it when Theresa's right!"

"Me too," Jo yelled. "But she's got it backward! She's trying to *help* Dr. Eve!"

"You think this Patrick guy is trying to expose Dr. Eve?"

"Who knows? We have to get back to the A-frame and find Theresa before she goes to see Dr. Eve!"

"She was long gone this morning," Caylin reminded her.

"You're right. But Dr. Eve's invite was for lunch. Theresa might be back already."

"Maybe if you wish real hard, that'll happen," Caylin muttered.

When they reached the A-frame, they leaped off the snowmobile and ran inside. They called out for Theresa, but there was no reply.

"She's not here," Jo said.

131

"That leaves only one option," Caylin replied.

Jo nodded. "Dr. Eve's château."

"Let's roll."

"Wait—leave the lyrics on the table. If we missed Theresa and she shows up here, I want her to see the song for herself."

Caylin nodded and tossed the lyrics to "Eve of Destruction" on the coffee table and zipped up her coat.

They headed out.

But once outside, they stopped dead.

Santino and Carlo waited for them, astride a pair of idling snowmobiles.

"Whoa," Jo blurted. "Hi, guys."

"You know, this *really* isn't a good time," Caylin said. "We're kind of busy."

"We thought perhaps you might like to go for a ride?" Santino suggested.

Jo chuckled. "Um, no thanks. Like she said. We're busy."

Carlo reached into his jacket and pulled something out.

Jo and Caylin gasped.

It was a gun.

"We insist," Carlo said menacingly.

"I—I'm sorry, Dr. Eve?"

"You seem very interested in something, Tish," the doctor said. "What is it?"

"This air. It's cold," Theresa said, putting her hand up to the vent.

Dr. Eve nodded. "There are vents leading up to the surface. Not much fresh air would get down here otherwise. Sometimes there are fumes."

"Fumes from what?"

"Many things. Natural gas. Chemicals. Anything you might find in a busy laboratory, Tish."

So the vents *did* lead down here, Theresa thought. Patrick must have figured that out.

"This must have been expensive to build," Theresa marveled. "Who paid for all of it?"

Dr. Eve cocked an eyebrow. "It was expensive. But I receive many grants from many governments. A lot of people would like to see me succeed in my work."

"I can imagine," Theresa replied. "If science paid half as well as pro sports, you'd be able to afford a castle."

Theresa heard a loud hiss. She followed the sound with her gaze. There was a large steel door in the far corner, behind some large equipment. A technician came through the door dressed head to toe in white. What struck Theresa as odd was the tech's full-head gas mask.

The tech shut the steel door, locked it down, and flipped a switch. It hissed again, then was silent.

"What's in there?" Theresa asked.

Dr. Eve paused. The tech passed them. The

way the man breathed in his gas mask, Theresa felt as if Darth Vader had just walked by. He disappeared into another chamber.

Dr. Eve cleared her throat. "It is a decontamination area."

"For what?"

Dr. Eve smiled. "Beyond that door are many computers and other supersensitive machines. We need a completely dust-free environment. That is why I can't show it to you."

"Oh. Why was that man wearing a gas mask?"

Tension crept into Dr. Eve's voice. "Sometimes we work with extremely hazardous chemicals. The technicians need to be protected."

"What kind of chemicals?"

"Do you always ask so many questions, Tish?" Dr. Eve demanded.

Theresa nodded. "I'm just curious. I thought you wanted me to ask questions."

Dr. Eve's expression darkened. "Unfortunately, curiosity is the curse of the scientist. That is the one lesson you will learn, Tish."

"Really?"

"Oh yes. Sometimes we learn more than is safe. And we get much more than we bargained for."

Dr. Eve sneered and slowly slid her hand into the pocket of her lab coat. Her face contorted strangely.

A wave of alarm shot through Theresa. Why did Dr. Eve suddenly seem so angry?

Dr. Eve kept reaching inside her pocket. Her sneer intensified.

Her eyelids fluttered.

She pulled a handkerchief out of her lab coat and violently sneezed into it.

"Gesundheit," Theresa said.

Dr. Eve honked and replaced the hanky in her pocket. "Thank you. I hope I'm not coming down with something."

Theresa relaxed. Dr. Eve's sneer was just a presneeze buildup.

"Shall we head back to the surface?" Dr. Eve offered. "You've seen quite a bit."

As they retraced their steps Theresa continued to thank Dr. Eve for the tour. "I know how private you are. Not everyone gets to see your lab the way I have."

"You're right, Tish. But your dedication and enthusiasm are obvious. In fact, you remind me a lot of myself when I was your age."

"Wow—thanks!"

They exchanged pleasantries all the way to the front door. Theresa felt as if she were floating.

"Now I really must say farewell, Tish," Dr. Eve said. "Be sure to keep in touch. I'd be happy to offer any recommendation letters you may need toward your education."

"Omigosh! That would be so great of you!"

"I would be more than happy to oblige."

Theresa shook the doctor's hand vigorously and thanked her once again. Before she knew it, she was outside, walking three feet above the snow-covered road toward town. She mumbled one supergeeky phrase over and over, not caring who heard her:

"Dr. Eve is the coolest person in the world!"

Santino and Carlo rode their snowmobiles at a steady clip, side by side, a Spy Girl perched behind each of them.

"This is ridiculous!" Jo barked. "What's with the guns? All you had to do was just ask us out."

"We're not laughing, Joan," Santino called over his shoulder. "If that's your real name."

"Hey, don't make fun of my name! I didn't pick it!" Jo grumbled, elbowing him.

"Oh, shut up for once," Santino replied.

"Kidnapping's a serious offense," Caylin added.

Santino shot Carlo a sly smile. "We're familiar with it."

"So you don't care about going to jail?" Jo asked.

"I should ask you the same question," Santino said. "We saw you on the doctor's surveillance video snooping that night of the party. You followed my brother to the door in the blackboard. Why would you do that, Jo?"

"I was looking for the bathroom!"

"Of course. We also saw the two of you talking to Rook last night at the club. Were you asking him where the bathroom was, too?"

"For your information," Caylin replied gruffly, "we were just getting his autograph."

"Were you getting his autograph at his home this morning as well?"

Jo and Caylin didn't answer.

"Finally: *silence!*" Carlo cheered.

"Yes, you are such big fans of Kristal, always asking if she's around, if we would know where she might be. Well, guess what, girls. We know *exactly* where she is!"

"Easy, Santino," Jo remarked. "Your ego is showing."

"Oh, be quiet." He grunted. "There is something going on that is bigger than all of you. And we're here to make sure that you never find out what it is."

Jo caught Caylin's eye. It was true about Dr. Eve! Caylin saw it, too. She reached down and tapped her boot. Then she jerked her thumb over her shoulder.

Jo knew exactly what she meant and nodded.

She grimaced, then forced herself to lean forward and softly kiss the back of Santino's neck.

"What are you doing?" he demanded.

"I'm just sorry things have to end this way between us, Santino," Jo said, pulling closer. She scowled, puckered up, and kissed him again.

The snowmobile slowed down ever so slightly.

That's when Jo leaned forward and said, "Consider that a good-bye kiss, chump!"

Then she and Caylin simultaneously flung themselves off the backs of the snowmobiles.

"Hey!" Santino yelled.

When they landed, they rolled on their backs, raised their boots in the air, and clicked heels.

The skis snapped out, and both Spy Girls launched themselves down the mountain.

"Faster, faster!" Jo hollered, looking behind her. "They're coming!"

"What I wouldn't give for a big fat snowboard!" Caylin screamed, crouching.

They shot down the slope full bore. The wind roared in their ears, but they could still hear the snowmobiles revving behind them.

"Head for those trees!" Caylin ordered. "They won't be able to keep up in there!"

Jo nodded and they turned hard for a stand of evergreens. She looked back. Santino and Carlo were right on their tails.

They plunged into the trees, cutting hard on their tiny skis. They lost a lot of speed, but then so did the twins.

"Are they still there?" Caylin called.

"Are you kidding?"

The snow deepened to over a foot. They sank in almost to their knees. They might as well have been skiing in a swamp.

"The skis are too small!" Caylin bellowed as the snowmobile engines revved louder. "We have to get out of this!"

They half-skied, half-stepped through the snow, eventually breaking out of the trees and ending up back on the open slope.

"Hurry!" Jo urged.

They picked up speed again. Behind them the twins burst out of the trees, catching some air. The sleds came down with loud thumps and continued the pursuit.

"If we can make it to the lodge, we have a chance," Caylin urged.

"That must be a mile away!"

"You have a better idea?"

"Yeah! Go home!"

"Come on, it's that way!"

"No, it's *that* way!"

Both pointed in different directions.

Jo cut left. Caylin slashed right.

And they collided head-on.

Both girls went down in a storm of snow and limbs. They rolled hard, tangled up like two dolls. A ski snapped off Jo's boot, clattering away. Snow coated their faces, invaded their mouths, choked off their breath. They coughed and sputtered.

Finally they came to a halt.

"Ouch," Jo mumbled.

"Ditto," Caylin said.

They heard the twins pull up and dismount. They opened their eyes.

Carlo aimed his gun at them. Santino rummaged around in his pocket.

"All right, signorinas," Santino said. "Let's try this one more time."

He brought his hand out, held up two pairs of handcuffs, and smiled.

The twins had added to Jo and Caylin's misery by putting ski masks on them, but backward so they couldn't see. Caylin assumed they were taken to Dr. Eve's château. That had been the general direction in which they'd been heading before they jumped off the sleds.

Caylin was taken off the snowmobile and roughly escorted inside. She could hear Jo complaining beside her. They all marched for a while, turned left and right several times, and then she heard a heavy door being opened in front of her.

"What's this?" Jo asked.

"Shut up," came Santino's voice.

The ski masks came off. Then they were shoved forward into a dark room.

The steel door clanged shut behind them.

It was pitch black.

"Cay?"

"Right here." She reached out and touched Jo's shoulder.

"Where are we?"

"My guess is the château. Somewhere inside the mountain."

"Figures."

Something moved off to their left.

"Did you hear that?" Jo whispered.

"I heard that."

"What was it?"

"Why don't you ask it?"

"I don't want to seem too forward," Jo replied. "I'm starting to think that flirting is one of my fatal flaws."

"What a breakthrough," Caylin muttered. "Is someone there?"

She was answered by a light, quiet voice, singing. A soft melody, slower than how Caylin had heard it before, but one that was immediately familiar.

"'Eve of Destruction,'" Caylin whispered.

The singing stopped.

"How do you know that?" came a gruff female voice. "That song hasn't been released yet! Did you bootleg it?"

Caylin's eyes had adjusted to the gloom, and she made out a shape approaching her. Short. Shapely. With what looked like long blond hair.

Jo let out a big, exhausted sigh. "Princess Kristal, I presume?"

Theresa walked back to the A-frame in a happy daze. The town buzzed around her, but she didn't notice any of it. Meeting Dr. Eve had been a dream come true for her, but actually talking with her and befriending her? That was totally unbelievable!

She was so wrapped up in her thoughts that she didn't notice the person who suddenly appeared next to her. He matched her step for step.

Finally he grabbed her arm.

Theresa jumped, but the guy had too firm a grip on her for her to back away.

"Hey, who—?" Her eyes widened. "Patrick!"

He nodded, moving her along. "Just keep walking."

"What do you think you're doing?" she demanded, trying to shake off his hand.

"It's time we had a heart-to-heart, Tish."

He guided her in another direction, away from the A-frame.

"Where are we going?"

"My place," he replied.

Theresa gazed into his face. Patrick refused to look at her. His expression was grim. There was no flirtation, no twinkle in his eye. Nothing.

Theresa remembered that he was most likely the enemy. He had something against Dr. Eve.

She had a feeling she was about to find out what.

13

Patrick had a tiny flat above a jewelry store on the outskirts of town. Three rooms—a living room with a sofa bed, a kitchen with a small collection of Vietnam-era appliances, and an unappealing bathroom. There was no TV or stereo, but ski equipment and magazines were scattered everywhere.

A card table was set up in the main room with several items Theresa recognized immediately: the same brand laptop that she had, with a ski-bum screen saver; three different passports from three different countries; and a variety of small surveillance knickknacks.

She glared at Patrick. "Who are you?"

"The question is, who are you?" he countered. "Has Dr. Eve hired you to protect her?"

Theresa blinked dumbly. "What are you talking about? I'm just here on vacation."

"Oh no, you're not. You're far too involved with that woman to be just a simple tourist. You've seen her several times. You followed me all over the mountain last night after telling me that you never wanted to see me again. You lied to me."

"I didn't expect to be caught," Theresa replied indignantly. "And what about you? Were you using me to get closer to Dr. Eve? All those lessons. All that attention. Did you think that I would lead you right to her?"

Patrick paused. "That has nothing to do with it."

"It has *everything* to do with it. It makes you ten times the liar and a hundred times more scummy."

Patrick blinked at that one. "Scummy?"

Despite her anger, Theresa felt herself blushing. "You know what I mean."

"The point is, Tish, that I wasn't using you. In case you hadn't noticed, I'd managed an invitation to Dr. Eve's that night without you. And I got on fine by myself up on that mountain." His expression softened slightly. "What does that tell you?"

Theresa sighed. "This is all just double-talk. If you weren't using me, then why did you spend all that extra time with me?"

He didn't answer at first. He looked away.

"Patrick?"

"You're infuriating."

"*Me? You're* the one running some kind of

scam! *You're* the one dragging me off by force!"

"I needed to know the truth about you. You can't just be here on vacation. There are too many coincidences."

"So you thought kidnapping me might solve everything."

"You're in no danger here. I won't hurt you." He swallowed hard. "I couldn't."

"You couldn't? What does that mean?"

"Because I care about you too much already!"

Theresa froze. He didn't just say that. He couldn't have said it. Because it couldn't be true. No one she ever had feelings for had returned them. And Patrick? For all of his deceptions, she knew he was her dream guy.

"Y-you *care* about me?"

"Isn't it obvious? You had me frightened to death last night because I thought you'd get shot. My head's been spinning since I met you. I'm lucky if I can concentrate five minutes at a time without thinking about you."

Theresa gulped. The belly butterflies had returned full force. "Really?"

He moved closer. Too close to be polite. "Really."

She gazed up into his eyes, and that was it. Her pulse pounded in her ears and her mouth went dry . . . which was bad . . . very bad . . . because she couldn't lick her lips . . . which was even worse . . . because he was about to . . . about to . . . kiss her.

Time stood still. She wrapped her arms around his neck and pulled him close. Every care left her. All she could think about was how wonderful his lips felt against hers.

Someone cleared his throat.

Impossible. No one else was in the dingy little apartment.

The kiss continued.

Someone cleared his throat again.

Patrick broke the kiss. "I hear you," he muttered.

"Hear who?" Theresa asked.

"Him," Patrick replied, pointing an angry finger at his laptop screen.

Theresa gasped. It was Uncle Sam!

But no—it wasn't Uncle Sam. Not quite. He didn't quite look the same. His face was distorted as always, but the shape was rounder, plumper. This man was heavier than Uncle Sam.

"Hello, Richard," he said, a perfect and proper British accent coming through.

"Richard?" Theresa shrieked.

"Hello, Jack," Patrick replied glumly. "Your timing is impeccable as always."

"Quite so, it seems. Found a friend, did we?"

"Yes."

"What is this?" Theresa demanded. "Who are

you working for? Are you a good guy or a bad guy or what?"

"I'm a good guy," Patrick said.

"Sometimes he is," the man called Jack interjected. "I don't know about now. Who is this tart, Richard, and why is she suddenly a part of this operation?"

Theresa's jaw dropped. "Excuse me? Tart? Did you just call me a tart?"

"Indeed I did."

"Listen up, you pixelated piece of—"

"Okay, okay!" Patrick blurted, trying to cover Theresa's mouth. Theresa shoved him away.

"Who is this person, Richard?" Jack demanded.

"I think I can answer that, Jack," came yet another voice.

"Uh-oh," Theresa moaned. "I think I'm in trouble."

"What?" Patrick asked, confused.

Theresa recognized this new voice. Knew it well—too well. She felt Uncle Sam's presence in the room even before his distorted face appeared next to Jack's, split screen.

"Sam, is that you?" Jack asked.

"Who else?"

"What's going on here?" Patrick said angrily. "Who *are* all you people?"

"My name is Uncle Sam, Richard. I'm Theresa's boss."

"Theresa? Who—what? *Her boss?*"

"Yes, Theresa's one of mine, Jack. Theresa, I'd like you to meet Union Jack, my counterpart in British intelligence."

"British intelligence?" she asked. She glared at Patrick. "You're a spy, too?"

"What do you mean, *too?*" Patrick asked, incredulous. "How many spies are in this town?"

"What is one of your operatives doing in one of my safe houses, Sam?" Union Jack wanted to know. "She has no clearance here."

"Theresa's working on Princess Kristal's disappearance," Uncle Sam explained. "At least, she's *supposed* to be working on it. Seems she's taken a shine to your boy here."

Theresa squirmed, smiling weakly at Patrick.

He nodded at her, smiling. "That sheds some light on a few things, doesn't it?"

Theresa nodded as well. "So if you're the good guys, what could you possibly have against Dr. Eve?"

"We've been investigating Dr. Eve Dankanov for several years now," Union Jack commented. "For what, I can't say. It's classified even for you, Sam. I apologize. But it occurs to me that your girl Theresa has actually been inside Dr. Eve's lab. She has earned Dr. Eve's confidence. She could be useful to us."

"Hey—," Theresa began.

"She has a mission of her own, Jack," Uncle Sam replied. "One that she's been *ignoring*. However, under the circumstances, she is the ideal candidate. You couldn't ask for a better covert operative when the operative has already infiltrated the enemy."

"I haven't infiltrated anything!" Theresa growled. "Dr. Eve trusts me because my interest in her work is real. Not because I have some twisted plot in mind. She showed me her work. She's totally dedicated to helping humanity. I'm sure of it."

"She was like that," Patrick said. "Once."

"Listen to Richard, Theresa," Jack urged. "Eve Dankanov has stepped off into another realm. One time, she was dedicated to helping solve the world's problems. But that is ancient history, I'm afraid. Trust us."

"You can't trust spies," Theresa retorted.

"Theresa, I am hereby ordering you to assist Richard in his investigation," Uncle Sam declared. "Do you understand?"

Theresa scowled. "This stinks."

"Duly noted," Uncle Sam continued. "But for once you will swallow your stubborn pride and follow orders. Work with Richard. You've been partners for two days, anyway. Simply continue. And round up the other Spy Girls as well. This mission is your new priority. Do you understand?"

"Yes, sir," Theresa said reluctantly. She wanted to tell him "I told you so," but thought better of it. She wasn't totally right, after all. A mission involving Dr. Eve was more important than finding Kristal. But she still refused to believe that her hero and mentor was an enemy of humankind.

It was impossible.

"All right, partners," Union Jack said. "Time to fly."

"Welcome to the team . . . Theresa," Patrick said, a wry smile playing across his face. He extended his hand. "It's a pleasure to be working with you. Officially, of course."

Theresa returned his smile. "Of course, uh, Richard."

He winked at her.

"All right, you two, that's quite enough of that," Union Jack scolded.

"You have a couple of Spy Girls to locate," Uncle Sam added. "Get cracking."

"Where does one find a pair of Spy Girls?" Patrick asked.

Theresa sighed. "That's a very good question."

"Well, before we get started, may I ask you a small favor?"

"What?"

He looked down at the floor. "May I continue to call you Tish?"

"If I can keep calling you Patrick," Theresa said with a smile. "We *are* spies, after all. Wouldn't want to blow our cover or anything."

"It's a deal, then."

"Mission accomplished, Jo," Caylin joked. "We found Kristal. Does this mean we can ski now?"

Jo snickered, bumping her head against the cinder block wall of the cell in frustration. "Cowabunga."

"Who are you people?" the princess demanded.

"Allow us to introduce ourselves," Jo replied. "I'm Jo. This is Caylin. And we're here to rescue you."

"Rescue me?" Kristal scoffed. "How can two little girls rescue me?"

"We're *not* little girls, *Princess*," Jo griped. "We're the same age as you."

"And you can start by telling us how you ended up in here," Caylin shot back. "What do you have to do with Dr. Eve?"

"No, I think *you* should tell *me* how you ended up in here," Kristal corrected. "Who are you working for?"

Jo sighed. Then she explained that they worked for "your basic, garden-variety intelligence-type organization." She told the princess how her mother had requested that the Spy Girls find her and return her home.

Kristal laughed bitterly. "You never would have gotten me to go. Even if you could have found me."

"We *did* find you," Caylin corrected.

"By accident," Kristal scoffed. "You probably spent all your time chasing after Rook."

Jo shot Caylin a tedious glance. "Why don't you tell your story now. We told you ours."

Kristal shrugged. "All I did was sing a song."

"'Eve of Destruction,'" Jo said.

"Yes. I sang the song for the first time in public at Rik's. Do you know Rik's?"

"We're familiar with it," Caylin replied dryly.

"I sang it so well, too. I sang it to Rook. He was so happy that night. Then I took my bows and went backstage. That's when they grabbed me."

"Who?" Jo asked.

"Those rude twins. Santino and . . ."

"Carlo," Jo finished.

"You know them?"

"We're familiar with them," was the reply, this time from Jo.

"Anyway, they took me at gunpoint. All of my security was still out front at our table. They weren't prepared for me to sing that night. It was a bit of a surprise, even for me. The champagne,

I guess. They brought me here. That's the story."

"But why?" Jo asked. "It doesn't make any sense for a world-class scientist to kidnap a princess. Does she want ransom?"

"No, it's nothing like that," Kristal replied. "I think Dr. Eve isn't sure what to do with me. It was kind of a misunderstanding, you see."

"What was?" Caylin asked. "The lyrics?"

"Yes. You heard the song?"

Jo nodded. "Rook played it for us. He wrote out the lyrics by heart."

Kristal grinned. "He can be so sweet sometimes."

"I think you need to get back to him soon," Caylin urged. "He's not bathing."

Kristal chuckled. "Yes, that's Rook. He's so lost without me."

"So what's with the lyrics?" Jo said anxiously.

"If you read them, you must have made the same connection that the twins did when they heard me perform at Rik's that night. Somehow, without knowing it, I made references to something Dr. Eve is working on. The twins thought I was some kind of spy, so they kidnapped me. Dr. Eve herself thought it was ridiculous, but she had me sing the song for her. I didn't sound very good, but it certainly shook her. I could see the anger in her eyes. Whatever she's working on, it must be top secret. And dangerous. Why else would she keep someone of my stature prisoner?"

Jo nodded, ignoring Kristal's ego trip. "That makes sense. But you had no clue that Dr. Eve was doing something nasty?"

"Not at all," Kristal replied. "It was a coincidence. Who knew I was such an ecological savant?"

"We have to find a way out of here," Caylin declared. "And soon."

"Oh, don't worry," Kristal replied. "Someone will come for me. If you two managed to find me, my bodyguards will certainly come soon. And no one will stop them."

Jo glanced at Caylin. Of course. Kristal lived in a different world, where people served her every wish. It was natural for her to think that way. Natural, and wrongheaded.

"I think we have a bigger problem than just getting out of here," Jo warned.

"What's that?" Caylin asked.

"Maybe the princess can answer that for us," Jo suggested. "Kristal, what's Dr. Eve working on that's so dangerous?"

"I don't know," Kristal whispered. "I really don't know. But it's bad. We're talking Armageddon, end-of-the-world bad."

I t was late afternoon when Theresa and Patrick
returned to the A-frame. When they entered,
Patrick whistled.

"This is your safe house?"

Theresa nodded. "Nice, huh?"

"It's ludicrous! You live here in pure luxury
while I toil away in squalor, sleeping on a lumpy
mattress and eating canned soup!"

Theresa shrugged. "We eat frozen pizza sometimes," she said lamely.

"So I see," Patrick muttered, picking up a dis-
carded box. "*Gourmet* frozen pizza with real
cheese. I think I need to have a word with Union
Jack regarding accommodations."

Theresa called out for Jo and Caylin. No answer.

"They're not here," Theresa said. "They've
been chasing Rook all over the mountain. They
could be anywhere."

"Hold it," Patrick said. He held up a sheet of
crumpled paper he found on the coffee table.
"Take a look at this."

Theresa read it. It was a set of lyrics to a song called "Eve of Destruction." A note was scribbled in the upper-left-hand corner: "T., check this out. Still think she's a goody-goody?" She recognized Jo's handwriting.

Theresa read the lyrics.

Slowly her eyes widened. Her heart sank. She desperately wanted not to believe it. But the evidence was mounting against her hero.

"Do you understand that?" Patrick asked.

Theresa barely heard herself. "Yes."

"You should know that the lines 'key to a worldwide door' and 'seals your doom' are pretty specific references. I can't tell you to what. But you have to trust me."

"There's that word again," Theresa muttered. "*Trust.* Trust should be a four-letter word."

Patrick turned her to him. "This is serious, Tish. I know you don't want to believe it, but it's true. I swear. And we have to do something about it."

Theresa nodded, swallowing the lump in her throat. "If it is true, then I know where Jo and Caylin are. They went looking for me at the château."

"Then that's exactly where we have to go," Patrick replied.

They waited for the sun to set. Then they set out for Dr. Eve's château. But instead of skis, this time they took the snowmobile.

"A beautiful house, new skis, new snow-mobiles," Patrick grumbled from behind her. "You girls have it made. I had to *buy* my skis."

"We're just lucky, I guess," Theresa replied, steering up the hill between trees. She was constantly aware of Patrick's body behind her. His strong arms around her. She sighed and tried to focus on the problem at hand.

But it wasn't easy.

They left the snowmobile a few hundred yards from the vents so the sound wouldn't attract any guards. They approached silently, using hand signals.

Finally the vents came into view. Patrick used his night vision goggles to make sure there were no guards nearby. There weren't, as far as he could tell. They stayed low and sneaked up to the first vent.

Warm air puffed out gently.

Patrick examined the cover to the vent. "It doesn't seem to be fastened," he whispered.

He carefully bear hugged it and lifted. The metal made a loud creaking sound as it came loose. To Theresa, it sounded loud enough to start an avalanche. She glanced around, but she saw no movement, no guards.

Patrick gently set the vent cover down in the snow and peered into the hole. It was definitely wide enough for a person to climb down. His hair fluttered in the warm breeze, and Theresa could see a golden glow on his face—there were lights below.

"This leads right into the lab?" he asked.

She nodded, immediately undoing her belt. Patrick paused, staring at her.

"Calm down, Mr. Bond," Theresa chided. "We're on a mission, remember?"

"Please don't call me that, old girl," Patrick retorted.

This time Theresa winked at him, and she began unwinding the climbing rope from her belt.

Patrick smiled and undid his own belt. His did the exact same thing. "Standard issue for mountainous terrain, right?"

"That's right," Theresa replied. "I just hope your government didn't cheap out on your rope the same way they did on your safe house."

"Very funny," Patrick remarked.

They tied the ropes end to end to be sure of the length, anchored them to a tree, and slowly lowered themselves into the vent.

The warm air felt good as it rushed up beneath her. It was like being in the barrel of a gentle blow-dryer.

Finally Theresa hit bottom, and Patrick was right there with her. A series of ducts led off in different directions. There was a vent right in front of them. They crouched down and peered through it.

"That's the main lab," Theresa whispered.

"Looks deserted," Patrick observed.

"It's night. Even Dr. Eve has to eat and sleep, right?"

Patrick slid his fingers through the steel grate and slowly worked it loose. After several seconds it popped outward. Patrick climbed out, dropped to the floor, and set the grate aside. He motioned for Theresa to follow, then replaced the grate.

The lab was indeed deserted.

"Is this the entire lab?" Patrick asked, fingering some equipment. "There's not much here."

Theresa remembered the air lock. A "decontamination" area, Dr. Eve had said. She pointed across the room at the door in the corner.

"That's supposed to be some kind of sterile room," Theresa said. "I wasn't allowed in there, and Dr. Eve got a little antsy when I asked her about it."

"Okay, then."

Patrick examined the mechanism. "It's a standard air lock. Supposedly all one has to do is press this button—"

The door let out a gigantic hiss that made Theresa flinch. *Someone* had to hear that!

"—and presto." The light above the door changed from red to green. Patrick unclamped the lock and swung open the door.

They stepped into a small, closet-size chamber with another door immediately ahead of them. This one was more modern-looking, made totally of thick Plexiglas.

Patrick closed the first door and clamped it. There was another loud hiss as the air lock compressed. Theresa's ears popped.

Then the light above the glass door went from red to green. Patrick opened it, and they stepped into a much larger lab.

"Whoa," Theresa whispered. "I never knew what state of the art meant until now."

All the equipment was pristine. The odor of fresh plastic was in the air, as if the computers had just been pulled from their boxes. And what computers! Some of them Theresa had never seen before. She was dying to turn one on and play, but there was no time.

"Over there," Patrick said, pointing. "That's what we want."

"The refrigerator? Why?"

"You'll see."

The refrigeration unit was massive, floor to ceiling, and sealed with a lock with a full-alphabet keypad. A tiny screen above asked for a password:

Patrick typed *Eve* and hit enter.

Access denied.

"Um, this could take a while," he muttered.

"Try *Mikhail 1515*," Theresa suggested.

"Really?"

"Just try it."

Patrick typed it in. The computer paused, then printed *access granted.* The lock clicked open.

"How did you know that?" Patrick demanded.

"That was the name of the lab Dr. Eve built in the space station." Theresa smiled. "What on earth would you do without me, Mr. Bond?"

Patrick waved a finger at her. "I'm warning you, old girl. . . ."

Theresa ignored him and pulled open the refrigerator, which was actually a liquid nitrogen deep-freeze containment unit. Steam from the nitrogen poured out of the shelving unit. Patrick waved aside the mist and put on one of his ski gloves. He reached in and plucked a small vial of a clear liquid from a collection of twelve.

He held it up to examine it. The heat of the room caused the glass to fog up. He wiped it away and showed Theresa.

"See that?"

"The liquid? What is it, poison?"

Patrick shook his head. "Look what's floating inside the liquid. In that tiny capsule."

"Uh-oh," Theresa whispered. "Looks like Dr. Eve discovered aspirin."

"This isn't funny, Theresa. That one capsule could contaminate the drinking water in all five boroughs of New York City."

Theresa's belly filled with lead. Her jaw dropped open. After all the posturing from Dr. Eve, all the lectures on purifying polluted drinking water . . . she had the ability to contaminate it!

"What *is* this stuff?"

Patrick shrugged. "No one knows for sure. It came back from space with her. Maybe she concocted it up there, maybe she just collected it up there. This is the closest anyone has gotten."

"Are you going to take it?"

Patrick nodded. "All of it."

He pulled a foot-long, flat steel case from a Velcro pocket in his thigh. He popped it open. A tiny rack hissed out on its own microwave of nitrogen mist. The case could hold twelve vials. Patrick started loading them up.

The air lock let out a massive hiss.

Theresa froze.

Someone was coming!

They had seconds before the outside door opened and they could be seen. Patrick had loaded only seven vials, but he slammed the refrigerator door shut, balancing the steel case in his free hand.

"Over here," Theresa whispered. "Under this table."

They slid across the floor and dived beneath a table next to the wall. If whoever came through that door didn't turn on many more lights, they would be pretty invisible.

The outside door clanked open. Someone stepped into the air lock.

Patrick struggled to close the steel case. In his haste a vial had wedged itself in the hinge. Theresa tried to help him free it, but he slapped at her hands, causing the unthinkable. . . .

The vial squeaked out from their fingers and flipped through the air.

Too far away to catch.

Too fast to stop.

All they could do was watch with wide eyes as their death hit the floor.

But the vial didn't break.

Theresa blinked.

The air lock hissed and opened. A white-coated lab tech walked in, someone Theresa had never seen before. He was younger, with shaggy long hair and black geek glasses. He held a clipboard and a cup of coffee.

Theresa and Patrick watched in horror as the vial slowly rolled across the floor toward the tech.

They didn't move. Didn't breathe.

The tech didn't notice it. He crossed the room, searched a table momentarily, and came up with a fancy-looking pen. Smiling and satisfied, the tech turned back toward the air lock.

Theresa relaxed. He only lost his pen!

Meanwhile, Patrick pried her claws out of his arm. She retracted them and sheepishly mouthed "sorry" to him.

The tech moved closer to the air lock.

And the vial still rolled.

Theresa spotted it. Saw the timing of the tech's steps. And clawed Patrick's arm again.

The tech's shoe came down on the vial with a crunch.

He cocked an eyebrow and looked down.

He saw what he did.

And he screamed.

"Move!" Patrick yelled. He threw aside the table and dove for the far wall. Theresa didn't see what he had in mind at first. Then she saw: gas masks.

A pair hung from a hook near the air lock. Patrick snagged them and hurled one at her. It hit her in the stomach and dropped to the floor.

Theresa held her breath.

The tech saw them, and his eyes registered fear and confusion. Then they focused on the far wall. Theresa saw it too. A big red alarm button.

He went for it.

Theresa scooped up the gas mask and strapped it on. Patrick grabbed her by the arm and dragged her toward the air lock. She saw tiny, smokelike wisps coming up from the crushed vial. Whatever was in it was now in the air.

She felt sick. What had they done?

They reached the air lock just as the alarm siren sounded. Patrick slammed the door shut and hit the button. Again the hiss. Again the ear pops.

In the lab the ceiling seemed to explode with jets of white steam. She'd read about something like that. A system for labs that worked with biohazardous gases. When a contaminate was unleashed, the jets cleaned the room.

She couldn't stop trembling. What had they let loose? Were they contaminated?

Something slammed into the glass door. Theresa screamed.

The tech.

He pounded limply on the door. His face had turned an ashen gray, as if the blood left his flesh. His teeth stood out yellow against his lips. His glasses hung on one ear.

Slowly he slid to the floor. Mouth agape. Hands clawed. Convulsing.

After another eternal moment, he lay still.

"We killed him," Theresa whispered.

"It was an accident," Patrick replied breathlessly. "He walked into a sterile biohazardous lab without a gas mask or suit? What was he thinking?"

"He was just getting his pen!"

"Would you rather it was you?" Patrick asked pointedly.

Theresa shivered, shaking her head.

"Remember that."

Suddenly the alarm shut down. The steel door clanked on its hinges.

"Uh-oh," Patrick whispered.

"Busted," Theresa replied.

The door creaked open. Dr. Eve, the twins, and three more security guards stared in at them.

"Tish," Dr. Eve said, shaking her head slowly. "You have *no* idea how disappointed I am."

They had all been rounded up in the front lab: Theresa and Patrick, along with Jo, Caylin, and Kristal. Theresa had run to embrace her friends when they'd been brought in, but the twins had separated them roughly.

The twins and the guards hung back, giving their boss the floor. Dr. Eve walked through the group of prisoners, speaking as she sized them up.

"So this is the best the world has to offer," she said haughtily. "Either the powers that be don't take my work very seriously or the intelligence recruiters of your countries have gone short on intelligence."

She focused this last remark on Theresa. The Spy Girl simply stared back, refusing to back down.

"You no doubt have something to say, Tish," Dr. Eve surmised. "By all means, indulge me."

Theresa took a deep breath and uttered only one short syllable: "Why?"

Dr. Eve grinned and leaned into her. "Why not?"

"That's a pretty childish answer," Theresa replied.

"To a childish question. A girl your age can't possibly understand what the future holds for all of us."

"Why not enlighten us," Jo suggested. "You love to lecture, after all."

Dr. Eve chuckled, but didn't bite.

"You're going to poison the world's water supply, aren't you?" Theresa asked.

Dr. Eve nodded.

"Why?"

"Why not?"

They all stared at each other for a moment.

"Should we start over?" Patrick asked. "You're going to contaminate the world's water supply, aren't you?"

Dr. Eve nodded. "I'll sum it up in one clean sentence so your short attention spans can absorb it."

"Talk about clichés," Jo muttered. "MTV hasn't destroyed us yet."

"It won't have the chance, if I have anything to say about it," Dr. Eve growled.

"So what's the deal?" Caylin asked.

"Put simply: A planet can support only a finite number of inhabitants."

"I can't believe it," Theresa said. "This is your idea of population control?"

"It's only temporary," Dr. Eve assured them. "We'll spread our little present around selected areas of the globe—areas that have the most to gain from population control—and let nature run its course. Human beings need to drink, after all. Then myself and a few key scientists shall live in space for a few months, formulating a cure."

Patrick nodded. "A cure that you've already discovered."

"Precisely," Dr. Eve replied. "We come back, population is down as well as global morale, and we administer my cure to the world's water supply. The human race goes on. And I live like a queen for the rest of my days."

"You're no queen," Kristal growled. "You don't even know the meaning of the word."

"Neither will you, Your Highness," Dr. Eve replied. "You'll be dead long before you can ascend the throne. Such that it is."

Kristal fumed but said nothing.

Dr. Eve walked over to Patrick. "I believe you have something that belongs to me."

She tore open the Velcro flap on his thigh pocket and withdrew the steel case holding the vials.

"Thank you very much." She turned to the

twins and the guards. "Gentlemen, why don't you take our guests back to their cell? And be sure to leave them a gallon of fresh water. You know, some of the experimental water from the lab. I'm sure as the days go by, they will become quite thirsty. It will be interesting to see who'll break down and drink it first."

Dr. Eve retrieved the last remaining vials from the refrigerator, placed them carefully inside the case, and marched toward the exit. The guards took a step toward them.

"Excuse me," Theresa called after her. "Dr. Evil?"

Dr. Eve turned and glared at her. "Yes, Tish?"

Theresa reached into her pocket and pulled out a small vial-shaped object. She made sure they all got a glimpse of it before she closed her fist around it and held it up.

"You forgot one," she said.

A wave of nervousness went through the room. Including the other spies.

Dr. Eve stood her ground. "I thought you were smarter than that, Tish. If you kill us all now, nothing good will come of it. But if you give me that vial, I can promise you a long life. You can grow up to be a scientist, too. Just like me."

"I'd rather die of thirst," Theresa spat.

She turned and whipped the object into the far corner as hard as she could.

The place went crazy. The armed guards screamed and ran for the exit. Dr. Eve hugged the steel case of vials to her chest and followed.

One of the twins punched a red alarm button, and the air was filled with sirens. The huge jets exploded from the ceiling, blinding them.

Everybody ran for the exit.

Theresa grabbed Patrick. He tried to force her gas mask back on her. She shook her head and screamed over the noise, "It was my lip balm! It wasn't a vial! We're not going to die!"

"What?" Jo called.

"We're not going to die!" Theresa repeated.

Everyone heard her this time.

Including the twins. They stopped in their tracks, turned, and glared.

"Uh-oh," Kristal said.

"Dr. Eve's getting away," Theresa urged, pushing Patrick toward the door. "Come on!"

"Go," Caylin told her. "We have a little unfinished business with our boyfriends here."

Theresa and Patrick ran around the far side of the lab and reached the door. The twins remained, eyeing Jo and Caylin.

"Alone at last," Santino said, cracking his knuckles.

"You wouldn't hit a girl, would you?" Caylin asked innocently.

"Never," Santino replied. "But in your case, I'll make an exception."

He lunged at her. Caylin sidestepped him, caught his fist, twisted it behind him, and bent him over. His face slammed against a hard lab tabletop.

Santino howled and fell to the floor, his nose gushing blood. He kept screaming, "Oh, my nose, oh, my nose," over and over.

"Your turn, Jo," Caylin said.

"What kind of girls are you?" Kristal asked from behind them.

"Spy Girls," Jo replied.

Carlo charged her. Jo let him. At the last second she grabbed his shirt and fell back, dragging him forward. Then she planted a foot in his gut, rolled backward on her back, and flipped him over her head. He landed hard, the air rushing out of him.

Jo stood, ready to face him again.

But as he stood, Kristal stepped forward and slammed a beaker over his head. Glass exploded everywhere.

Carlo dropped like a sack.

"That's for being rude," Kristal announced, dusting off her hands.

"Amen, Your Majesty," Jo replied with a grin.

Theresa and Patrick sprinted out the front door of the château. It was hard to see in the failing light, but they caught a glimpse of Dr. Eve turning the far corner near the garages.

"That way!" Theresa ordered.

Suddenly the air was shattered by the roar of an engine. As Theresa and Patrick rounded the corner, Dr. Eve sped off on a snowmobile.

"We have to catch her!" Theresa said.

"There's another one," Patrick said, pointing. "Get on! I'm driving this time."

"Chauvinist," Theresa growled.

Patrick turned the ignition and revved the engine. "Not at all. I've seen you drive, that's all."

"Hey—"

Patrick cut her off by peeling out. They flew up the hill, following Dr. Eve's trail.

The lights of the château quickly faded, and the further out they headed, the darker it became. All they had to guide them was the headlight and the fresh path carved by Dr. Eve's sled.

Patrick gunned the machine for all it was worth. The wind whipped Theresa's hair, stinging her cheeks and lips.

"I think my face is frozen!" she screamed.

"Just hang on! I see her!"

Theresa looked over Patrick's shoulder and saw a dim red taillight up ahead.

"Where is she going?" Theresa asked.

"I know exactly where," Patrick replied. "There's a reservoir not far from here."

"Oh no! It probably serves the whole valley!"

"Not just that," Patrick said. "They bottle the water, too. They sell it all throughout eastern Europe."

Theresa's stomach tightened. "She'll kill millions!"

"That was her point, yes," Patrick replied.

Gradually the terrain flattened out. They were topping the mountain. In front of them was a huge flat expanse of white.

The lake.

"Is it frozen?" Theresa asked.

"I hope so!" Patrick blurted as they launched off a short rise. Theresa's stomach lurched, and they landed hard on the ice.

It didn't crack.

Patrick went full throttle and gained ground on Dr. Eve. In seconds they were pulling alongside her sled.

"Stop!" Theresa called.

Dr. Eve snarled and pulled something from her coat.

Theresa gasped. "Gun!"

Dr. Eve fired. The bullet sailed over their heads, but the sound made Patrick swerve. They slammed into Dr. Eve's snowmobile violently.

Plastic shattered. Engines revved.

And Theresa felt the whole world pitch sideways.

All of them hit the ice. Theresa caught a glimpse of a snowmobile flipping in midair. Patrick was nowhere. Dr. Eve spun across the ice in front of her.

Finally they all came to rest.

Theresa just lay there, panting, wondering if she was really alive. She must have been because the ice was *freezing* under her.

She raised herself up on one elbow and looked around. Dr. Eve was a few yards to her left. To her right, a capsized snowmobile. That was all she could see.

She turned back to Dr. Eve. She was moving. Blood trickled from a cut on her forehead. But Theresa stared at her hands. She was fumbling with the opened steel case, collecting spilled vials off the ice and placing them safely inside.

Theresa crawled toward her. She tried to count the vials as Dr. Eve picked them up.

Seven . . . eight . . .

She got to eleven and slammed the steel case shut. She stuffed it inside her coat.

"That's only eleven," Theresa gasped, fumbling toward her on the ice. "Where's the other one?"

Dr. Eve grinned. She held up her hand and showed it to her.

"Don't!" Theresa begged. "Don't drop it!"

"I have to," Dr. Eve replied. "Don't you see that?"

The ice shifted beneath them. A long, loud creak came up like the howl of a wolf.

Dr. Eve locked eyes with Theresa for a split second, triumph spreading across her face.

Then the ice caved in.

Theresa dove forward with it, simultaneously slamming into Dr. Eve and reaching for the vial.

She felt it slip from her fingers, and she and the doctor both fell into the water.

It seemed as if a hundred knives stabbed Theresa. The water was beyond cold, beyond anything she could ever imagine. She grabbed at everything, praying to find the vial, picking up sharp chunks of ice. Feeling her hope dwindle as she slowly sank into the frigid depths.

This was it.

She was going to die.

She and millions of others.

Because she failed.

Suddenly there were hands on her, pulling her up.

She was out of the water, breathing air. But she was paralyzed. Legs stiff, fists balled tight.

She was so cold . . . so cold.

"Tish, it's Patrick. You're all right. Do you hear me? You're all right."

"The vial," Theresa mumbled. "I lost it."

Patrick grinned and put his lips to her ear. They were so warm.

"The vial's in your hand, Tish," he said, holding her fist up to show her.

Sure enough, there it was, frozen to her glove.

"Ha . . . I caught it," was all she could say before she blacked out.

As the music faded, the applause got louder. Kristal raised a fist and saluted the crowd at Rik's one last time. Then she marched backstage and leaped into Rook's waiting arms.

It was a kiss for the ages.

"That is so sweet," Jo remarked.

"Being a VIP is so sweet," Caylin replied, sipping her carrot-apple-celery cocktail and fingering the backstage pass around her neck. "I could get used to this."

"We have a whole week," Jo countered. "We could do a lot of damage in a week."

"Look how much damage we did in three days!" Caylin cheered.

"I know!" Jo mimed wiping her brow. "But boy, that was a close one. When we got back to the A-frame and called Uncle Sam, we'd just scraped the seventy-two hour mark."

Caylin raised an eyebrow. "I have a feeling we'd have gotten our week's vacation, anyway."

Jo nodded. "It's not like we don't deserve it or anything. I mean, in addition to saving the world's water supply and stuff, we not only found Kristal—"

"And reunited her with her boyfriend—"

"But we reunited her with her family, too," Jo finished, smiling as Queen Cascadia embraced her daughter, then Rook. "Looks like the royals might be loosening up a bit."

"Well, now they know Rook's a good guy," Caylin mused. "He's cleaned up his act, and he helped us find Kristal. Now they know he has her best interests at heart."

Jo sighed. "Isn't it romantic?"

"Oh, it's the *most*, my *deah*," Caylin drawled.

They clinked glasses and celebrated.

"Speaking of romantic, where's Theresa?" Jo asked.

"Where do you think?" Caylin replied, gesturing over at the corner.

"That was a great show," Theresa said with a shy smile. "And I mean that, really. No lie."

"It was," Patrick replied. He leaned his shoulder against the wall and brought his head down close to hers. "Thanks to you, the world is safe for rock and roll once again."

She smiled, shivering. She still felt so cold sometimes. But they said that it would go away eventually. She'd just have to wear a lot of sweaters in the meantime.

"Are you okay?" Patrick asked.

Theresa nodded. "It's not every day I go swimming with the frozen fish sticks."

"You'll be fine."

"Yeah, but it'll take years to live down Jo and Caylin's *Titanic* jokes. So there were icicles in our hair—so what? We don't look a thing like Kate and Leo!"

Patrick laughed at first, but then his expression turned serious once again.

It had been doing that all night.

"You're leaving, aren't you?" she asked.

He nodded.

"I thought so."

"Now that Dr. Eve is in the hands of the proper authorities, I have another assignment. I catch a plane in an hour."

Theresa wanted to reach out and hold him, but instead her hands stopped short and merely straightened his collar. "You take care, Mr. Bond. You hear?"

Patrick smiled and nodded. "Your wish is my command, old girl."

He swept her into his arms and kissed her. A proper spy kiss that put Kristal and Rook to shame. It was a kiss Theresa would never forget.

She ignored Jo and Caylin's catcalls.

"Good-bye, Theresa."

"Good-bye, Richard."

He strode away. But before he hit the exit, he turned back to her.

"Perhaps our paths will cross again," he suggested. "The club we belong to is a pretty exclusive one. Just don't burn out on me."

Theresa grinned. "Not a chance," she whispered as she watched him disappear behind the door.

She stood alone for a moment and sighed. Then she took a deep breath and joined her fellow Spy Girls near the refreshment table.

Jo wrapped Theresa in a conciliatory hug. "Them's the breaks, lover girl," she said. "You going to be okay?"

"I think so," Theresa murmured. But she wasn't quite sure.

"We're sorry we doubted you, T.," Caylin offered as she lightly punched Theresa on the shoulder. "Let's never fight again. Promise?"

"Promise," Theresa replied with a smile. "So, how's the grub back here, anyway?"

"Fit for a princess," Jo quipped. She held up a gold foil-wrapped box. "But I think *this* little item has your name all over it."

"Chocolate!" Theresa gasped. "Ohhh, just what I need right now." She tore into the box. "Wait— there's no chocolate in here."

"What?" Jo and Caylin replied in stereo.

Theresa held up a package of Brazil nuts and a CD of samba music. "Can anyone say, 'Uncle Sam was here'?"

Caylin smiled. "I bet I know what this means."

"Whoo-hoo!" Jo cheered. "Rio de Janeiro, here we come!"

About the Author

Elizabeth Cage is a saucy pseudonym for a noted young adult writer. Her true identity and current whereabouts are classified.

SPY GIRLS

The tantalizing trio is *spy*ing down to Rio!
They're shaking their groove things in Brazil's
spiciest clubs while dishing the dirt on a major
drug-smuggling operation. Only Diva, the hip,
young owner of Rio's hottest nightspot, can help
the Spy Girls get around in the underground.
But she's also the daughter of the man who
killed Jo's father! Jo wants justice by any means
necessary, even if it destroys the mission—and
Diva's world. When her thirst for revenge turns
deadly, will Jo be forced to go solo?

**It's all about action, Jackson!
Go on with your bad self
and check out
Spy Girl mission #5:**

DIAL "V" FOR VENGEANCE

**Coming
May 1999**